This new book was pre
East Anglia Children's
by Bob Able, the autho

Please give it back to a charity shop when you have read it
so that it can be sold again to make more money
for worthwhile causes!

The Smug

Bob Able

Copyright © 2024 Bob Able

All rights reserved

The characters and events portrayed in this book are fictitious. Any similarity to real persons, living or dead, is coincidental and not intended by the author.

No part of this book may be reproduced, or stored in a retrieval system, or transmitted in any form or by any means, electronic, mechanical, photocopying, recording, or otherwise, without express written permission of the publisher.

This book was published to mark 100 days since Russia's invasion of Ukraine, and is dedicated to all the Ukrainians who were displaced or killed in this conflict.

CHAPTER 1

In the initial months since the plastic sign-maker's franchise went bust, we of the Smugglers' Rest confidently predicted that, once a buyer for the business was found and the rest of the slightly garish new sign lettering could be delivered, the scaffolding would be removed.

Whilst the timescale remained uncertain, before Mrs Glendenning, our ever-optimistic hostess was admitted to hospital, we allowed time to slip by and proceeded to peer out at the world under the truncated banner reading 'The Smug' as if nothing was wrong.

But that was all history now. A tall and aggressive Japanese Knotweed plant had broken through the tarmac and twined itself confidently around one of the uprights of the scaffolding, and lesser weeds are winning over the spaces beneath. That element of the lettering of the bold new sign which had been erected already had a patina of bird muck and rain-streaks, and the front of the building was partly concealed in a sort of leafy decay.

Now inured to the teasing, we had accepted our situation, and even referred to our preferred hostelry as 'The Smug' amongst ourselves now. We found the joke quite fitting, in a way, and hunkered down to make the best of it as yet another temporary landlord, or 'manager', was installed by the brewery.

At least the beer kept flowing, even though the prices charged did inexorably creep up, and the conversation inevitably touched upon the pain in the wallet we all felt with each new incremental rise.

But we were not disheartened; at their roots the hardened regulars, even in a 'themed' seaside pub, out of season, rarely are. Curmudgeonly and opinionated, certainly; and prone to what used to be called 'gallows humour', but never downhearted. At least not until closing time.

'The Smug' looks out on a little parade of shops one row back from the seafront and rubs shoulders with a betting shop on one side, and a public carpark on the other.

The shops opposite were once the vibrant heart of this seaside community but, as so often happens, as the demographic of these places change, now offered little to the passer by. Since the post office had closed down, the only remaining chain store was the Oxfam shop. The other premises were occupied by a tawdry collection of shops selling tat, new or secondhand. There was also one still hopefully offering colourful plastic buckets and spades for the dwindling number of people prepared to sit on the pebbly beach. Some were still brave enough to risk a dip in the sluggish grey and chilly sea, between the island of floating plastic waste and the green and slimy outfall pipe, which gushed unpleasant smelling liquid when it rained.

As a place to retire it was very attractive a few short years ago.

We of The Smug have watched the changes from the warmth of our open plan, fake oak beamed, dimly lit bar room with a gloomy resignation.

Lately we can sit in our chosen spots at the once busy tables, where not that long ago we would not have found space. But since The Smug stopped serving food to any great extent and, after the Covid pandemic, when our bar stools were removed, we now had our choice of chairs and tables as we took our ease.

Of course, if you were brave enough, you could still find something to eat at The Smug.

The curved glass servery cabinet at one end of the bar still offered a plate of scotch eggs arranged in a pleasing pyramid, and some plastic wrapped pies from a well known manufacturer, arranged to conceal their 'use by' dates until they made the final journey through the microwave, and onto the plate of any unsuspecting passer-by impecunious enough to order one of them.

But there were rarely any passers-by now. Those of us who continued to populate the place knew that the food offerings were to be avoided and that sustenance, if required, could be found at the fish and chip shop facing the sea, next to the amusement arcade, or the Indian take-away adjacent to the former Lifeboat Inn, now boarded up and displaying a forlorn-looking faded 'For Sale' sign.

But we of The Smug did not become 'regulars' here for the food or the artificial 'Tiffany' lampshade lit ambiance. What kept us coming back was the conversation.

What sustained us was the sparkling repartee of oft told anecdotes and bawdy jokes, of the sort now frowned upon in the world beyond and outside. As did the wide ranging political opinions and sometimes unrealistic, and no-doubt painful, options as to how those currently in control should be dealt with, once power was assumed by The Smug's small collection of vocal pocket revolutionaries.

This was a place of ideas and inspirations. Unfulfilled hopes were revisited, and fantastical fictitious appointments were made with imaginary members of the opposite sex, or those whose pictures appeared in the various newspapers and periodicals, which were refreshed most days, and available for the customers to peruse as they purchased their drinks.

For gentlemen of a certain age, The Smug was a refuge and a comfortable place to mount a defence against an increasingly perplexing world. Here they could rail against the changes they saw and the frustrations they felt, in the secure knowledge that what happened in The Smug, stayed in The Smug.

But the Brewery had decided to close it down.

CHAPTER 2

Barry Beeching had worked for the brewery for nearly thirty years.

The first eight or ten had been spent as one of a team of 'acquisition managers' who, at a time of expansion for the industry, had the job of acquiring pubs and restaurants for the company to grow their burgeoning 'steakhouse' business.

Then, as the fortunes of the pub trade went into reverse, his job role changed, and his task now was to try to find buyers for the less viable properties the brewery owned, in a dwindling marketplace. He was still called an 'Acquisitions Manager', but was concerned solely with disposals, in the current trading conditions.

One of his early acquisitions, back in the day, had been The Coach and Horses, which was re-branded as 'The Smugglers' Rest', re-vamped into a steak-house and stamped with the company's brand and signature style of decor.

The decor remained the same today, although there had been 'improvements and modernisations' along the way, such as a new kitchen and repeated work to the beer pumps and cellar. The carpet in the bar, however, which followed the brewery's house style, was now over ten years old, and was showing its age.

The building originally had three separate bars, but had been opened up into one large dining area, with a wide bar and servery, as soon as the brewery completed their purchase. There was also a separate 'off-sales' room when the pub was built, which created a single storey link under a lean-to roof between the pub and the bookmakers premises next door. Although it had not served its original purpose for many decades, this part of the building was designed as an off-licence for customers to purchase drinks, including beer, in bottles, without going into the bars. That section of the pub was now incorporated into the kitchens and the street doorway was used to make deliveries to avoid the need to go through the bar and restaurant.

The 'front of house' area was adorned with oak beams, some of which were fake and served no purpose, swathes of thick rope above the bar, and a motley collection of crab pots, bits of fishing nets, brass lamps, rusty anchors and all the sort of coastal paraphernalia the brewery imagined would evoke a seafaring theme.

There were wooden dividers, with artificial leaded

glass panels depicting sailing boats and roiling seas, in-between carefully planned collections of tables, which could accommodate parties or intimate dinners. The lighting, provided for the most part by those artificial 'Tiffany' lampshades, probably plastic, and now concealing LED bulbs, was deliberately kept low, which hampered cleaning but did add 'atmosphere', if you were susceptible to that sort of thing.

Generally, it was dated but comfortable, but it had lost its purpose and became a financial liability when the management, in the face of Covid, yet another economic recession and limited foot-fall, decided to stop serving food and close the kitchens.

While remaining open for business 'The Smugglers' Rest' had been quietly offered for sale to the trade as a going concern for nearly three years now, with no takers.

-oOo-

One of the more accomplished patrons of 'The Smug' was Major Peter Harris, now a widower.

When he retired from the army as a tank commander (now moderately deaf, a common problem for tank crew, he informed us), he and his wife moved in with his mother-in-law, in her spacious bungalow. It backs onto those newish houses where the market gardens used to be.

The mother-in-law needed care, which the Major's

wife provided until she contracted an aggressive form of cancer and died some eight years previously. After that, Major Harris himself took over the caring responsibilities until his mother-in-law passed away.

She was a remarkable old lady, who almost to the very end compiled crosswords for national newspapers such as the Daily Telegraph; and in the war, had worked at Bletchley Park, the secret facility where the best of the British Intelligence Services were sent to work.

When asked, Major Harris cited the 'Official Secrets Act', tapping the side of his nose, and explained that she never discussed what she did there, but she spoke fluent Russian and taught the language to Major Harris for fun, while he looked after her in her declining years.

When she died, some property deeds and a legal contract were discovered. They revealed that many years before, not long after moving into her bungalow, she had purchased a half share in the market garden behind her property, and eventually bought out her partners and sold the land to the developers who built the little estate that stands there today.

It was never mentioned directly, but we of The Smug got the impression that with no other family, she had left Major Harris quite a bit of money as well as the bungalow he continued to live in.

On the main road a handful of miles from The Smug, there is one of those 'hand car washes', operated now, as so many are, by Ukrainians. They seemed to have taken over from a group of gimlet eyed Afghans, who had much to learn about the art of dealing with customers, as well as cleaning cars, and for whom trade dwindled and eventually stopped. We of The Smug believed that the new individuals working there might have been immigrants, and there was some discussion about whether they might in fact be illegal. It was well known, after all, that a couple of years before, an overloaded boat of immigrants had made it to the pebbly beach by the former Lifeboat Inn, and only half a dozen of those aboard were caught by the local Coastguard and turned over to the police.

We all agreed, however, that the people running the car wash were always polite and respectful and whilst they did not speak much English, they did a very good job of cleaning cars.

Most of the incoming Ukrainians who remained in the district lived with their families in what used to be the Seaview Guest House, near the Indian Take-away. It was now run by the Council, and the residents pretty much kept themselves to themselves.

Major Peter Harris got involved with a charity who, working alongside the Local Council, tried to find those people permanent housing, sorted out their immigration papers, and when that was done, tried to find them work. They also sought to befriend them on behalf of the community, and offered what assistance they could to help them to settle and integrate. And they redoubled their efforts when the Government said that these particular refugees should be allowed to stay.

Major Harris made himself very popular as an interpreter, particularly with the Ukrainian families because he spoke excellent Russian, and without any external assistance or payment he arranged to give them English lessons. Some thirty-four percent of Ukrainians speak Russian as a first language, he informed us, and pretty much all of the population speak some Russian as well as Ukrainian, so his services were gratefully received and much in demand.

For his lessons he used the Residents' Lounge in the Homely House retirement flats, behind the former Post Office and opposite the Funeral Home, where several of we of The Smug live.

This room was only used about twice a year for a cancer charity coffee morning, or for tea and cake after a funeral, when one of the residents passed away. Following the cut-backs, now that we no longer had an 'on-site' warden, or 'House Manager' as they were called, we just had the orange pull-cords to summon help via a remote call-centre.

Major Harris just took over the room and gave his English lessons twice or sometimes three times a week. He chose not to trouble the Management in their office many miles away, with the formality of making bookings. None of the Residents seemed to find the need to tell the Management about this unauthorised use, so no-one bothered them, and they didn't make any mess or noise, so the Residents just smiled and left the Major to it.

Several of the flats in Homely House had been put up for sale or offered to rent as and when residents died, and now nine or ten were empty. Major Harris did approach the Management Company that owned the building about that, and asked if they could be rented to the Ukrainian families he was working with, so that they did not have to live in a guest house, sometimes five or six to a room.

The down-at-heel accommodations they occupied in the Government funded hotel rooms at the former Seaview Guest House were unsuitable places to bring up children, to say the least, and the building had been due to be demolished before the Government's urgent need for somewhere to put the refugees gave it a stay of execution.

Major Harris received a curt reply from the Management company in charge of Homely House, stating that any residents had to be over sixty-five years of age and have sufficient means to pay the expensive and much complained about 'maintenance charges' the flat-owners had to pay.

He wrote back and asked if an exception to the age restriction could be made on humanitarian grounds for these displaced people, if a charity paid all their bills, but he never received a reply.

-oOo-

One or two of us had been to visit Gloria Glendinning in hospital. As the landlady of 'The Smug' she held the licence to sell intoxicating liquor, of course, and although she was on long term sick leave, the brewery, which owned the premises, could not move without her.

She was optimistic that she would be able to return and run the pub again, although that seemed unlikely. But in her dealings with the brewery she was robust and determined, and made it clear that she would not give up the licence unless she really had to.

As a result, the brewery had to appoint a succession of 'Temporary Managers' to run the pub and keep we of The Smug afloat with our favourite tipples. Those appointed to fill these roles had varying degrees of success.

The first, a grudging and miserable middle aged northerner who did not last long was replaced by a young couple who had little idea of what to do.

They were swiftly replaced by an immensely fat semi-retired publican named Jack, with Nan, his thin and nervous wife, who stayed for quite a while. He was very jolly and amenable, but we quickly realised that we had to check our change carefully as several mistakes were made in the cut and thrust of a busy lunchtime session. When these errors came to light, the shortages were quickly corrected, with an apology and perhaps a comment about needing new glasses. But their sojourn at The Smug came to a sudden end, when one day they simply did not turn up for work.

On that dramatic morning, we of The Smug who prefer an early libation to set us up for the day, were left standing outside in the cold facing a locked door.

On that occasion, Gazza, a retiree originally from London, came into his own and telephoned the brewery demanding action.

While we took shelter in the Resident's Lounge in Homely House and made do with tea while we awaited events, the men from the brewery dispatched Barry Beeching, in his company car, to meet a locksmith at the premises and effect an entry. He was joined there later by yet another 'Temporary Manager' in the form of Doris Smith, a Londoner, from Hackney, who it transpired had once lived just around the corner from our own Gazza, before she too retired to the coast.

Doris was employed by the brewery on a sort of part-time 'emergency call-out' basis to cover incidents like this, which she informed us were actually quite common.

Doris was lovely, and efficiently got the pub up and running in time for the early evening shift. She was rapidly joined by Mike and Emma who were to become our next 'Temporary Managers' and remained in post throughout the upheaval which was to follow.

Having settled them in, Doris returned home, there to await her next emergency call-out, and things at The Smug settled down.

-oOo-

Mike and Emma had been living with their daughter nearby, having been made homeless following a fire at their own pub somewhere in Hertfordshire.

They showed us pictures, and it was plain to see that open fires and a thatched roof, possibly with elderly wiring, had been a combination best avoided.

Emma, who was a comfortably built cheerful sort, with a ready smile, had sustained burns in the fire when she tried to rescue her cat. One arm bore the scars of her heroism, but Augustus, now everyone's friend in The Smug, was apparently none the worse for wear, and paused for strokes and fussing at regular intervals as he carried out his patrols of the bar.

Mike was from Derbyshire, and had a very dry sense of humour. He knew his business however, and kept an excellent cellar. He even disposed of the aging pies and gave the ancient scotch eggs a decent burial. He replaced them with offers of sandwiches, toasted, if required, and occasionally the smell of bacon rolls being prepared greeted early visitors.

Mike told us that, if he could persuade the brewery to

let him use the kitchen, he hoped to be able to offer cooked breakfasts in the near future. A prospect we all viewed with relish.

But then the letter arrived from the brewery stating that The Smug was to be closed down.

-oOo-

CHAPTER 3

Mike came to sit with us that morning, clutching two letters on the Brewery's headed paper.

The first was the official notice of intention to close The Smug, signed by Barry Beeching. Bizarrely the second was from someone signing herself as H. Pople (Ms.) confirming that, if Mike and Emma were prepared to pay for recommissioning the kitchen and acquiring the necessary gas and electricity safety certifications, they were welcome to prepare and serve cooked breakfasts. There was also a complicated formula to be used to calculate how much was due to the brewery from the sales of any food, which caused Mike to scratch his head.

The letter from Barry Beeching asked if Mike and Emma could attend a meeting to discuss the timetable and procedure for running down and closing the pub, and suggesting a date for the meeting.

'Emma was really upset,' he said, handing round the letter. 'We had put every penny we had into our last pub and lost everything, literally everything, in the fire. We even had to borrow some money from our daughter to buy clothes, and that. Been there ten years, we had. We only got this place because we could start immediately, and Emma was beginning to think that, even if we could only be managers rather than landlords of our own place, at last she had a chance to rebuild our lives, like. And now this. If we have to start all over again I'm not sure Emma can take it ...'

When Mike went back to tend the bar, those of us present sat in stunned silence for a while. Even Augustus the cat sensed something was wrong and sat on the chair at the head of the table swishing his tail.

Major Harris was the first to speak.

'I don't know about you chaps,' he said, 'but I'm not ready to give up on 'The Smug' quite yet. There must be something we can do.'

-oOo-

At the meeting, Barry Beeching explained that the pub's bar stocks would be run down over the next three months, and then the building would be boarded up and put on the open market.

Fortunately the cellars had just been re-stocked when the letter arrived, so the brewery calculated that it would take up to three months to sell off the stock and close the bar. It could be sooner, but it could not be later, he explained, as the property was scheduled to be auctioned off.

For Mike and Emma, who had only recently moved into the living accommodation above the bar, it was also an eviction notice. In three months time they would be homeless again, unless the brewery could find them another pub to take on as 'Temporary Managers.'

When Emma asked, Barry admitted that was highly unlikely because most of the 'dead wood' had now been sold off and they currently had no empty pubs.

The brewery might be able to give them some work as 'holiday cover' he said, but it would only be a week here, and a week there, and would depend on appointments made by the Area Finance Director, rather than him.

At that point Emma burst into tears.

-oOo-

'Biggles' Lancaster only had one eye, but he winked at us now as he made his suggestion, a few days later.

'I bin thinking,' he said. 'If we put it about that breakfast was being served up at The Smug each day, half the old sprouts from Homely House and loads of folk from the town will form a queue, if it is cheap enough.'

We of The Smug try to keep an open mind and turned to look at Biggles, as he paused to sip his pint. He may not be Mensa material, but the retired school caretaker did sometimes string comprehensible sentences together.

'Emma n' Mike have got the insurance money coming from their old pub, like, but they ain't got it yet, so ...' We waited as he took another gulp of beer. 'So I was wondrin' see. If we had a bit of a whip round to raise the money to clean up the kitchen an' get these here certificates to say the gas and that is safe, maybe they could raise a bit of money to tide themselves over, like...'

'Biggles,' said Gazza, in amazement. 'That is actually not a bad idea.'

'It is a very fine idea,' said Major Harris, setting down his empty glass and signalling to Mike at the other end of the bar that he required another scotch and soda. 'And while we are on the subject, may I add a few thoughts of my own?'

All eyes turned to the Major, as he cleared his throat and prepared to lay out his ideas.

-oOo-

Augustus, the cat, had taken to living at The Smug like a duck to water, and made friends with all the customers.

He was also often to be seen around the back of the fish and chip shop, next to the amusement arcade, where eye witness reports had it that he had seen off the resident tom-cat in a running fight, and proclaimed himself as the master of the district.

The fish and chip shop was the weekly haunt of several of the refugee families who lived in the former Seaview Guest House who, it was rumoured, had no proper cooking facilities. They were related in some way to the Ukrainians who worked at the hand car-wash up on the main road, who turned up and bought their meals on payday.

The roly-poly man who ran the establishment took a generous view when it came to serving these impoverished people and usually charged them half price, or even nothing at all when the food was being bought by the mothers for their children.

There was very little waste, but when there was, Augustus could always be relied upon to find and demolish any edible morsels which might be left over.

As such, he made great friends with the children, and one in particular who, despite the language barrier, managed to make the chip shop proprietor understand that her family had had a cat that she loved very dearly, who got left behind when they had to leave their home country.

In order to ensure that Augustus put in an appearance when this little girl visited the shop, once a week on a Friday, with her mother and baby brother, the roly-poly shop owner kept a handy supply of fish heads and cooked offcuts in the fridge. Augustus soon learned the routine and always made himself available to spread a little comfort and happiness.

-oOo-

'I've been doing a little research,' began the Major. 'Have any of you fellows ever heard of a "Asset of Community Value", by any chance?'

There was a general shaking of heads.

'Tha' Headmistress said I was an asset when I retired …' said Biggles, but quickly subsided into silence.

'I'm not sure if you remember, but Brenda, my late wife, did a spell as a Parish Councillor not long after we moved here, and when I finally got round to clearing out some of the mountain of paperwork that had generated recently, I found a copy of an update sent from a Government office to the Council Clerk about a new scheme whereby a building or a playing field or what-not could be registered as one of these "Community Assets", if they could make a good enough case for it, which might stop it being sold off.'

The Major had our full attention now, and even Augustus the cat sat up straight and appeared to follow his every word.

CHAPTER 4

Augustus did not have it all his own way at The Smug. Occasionally customers would bring in dogs.

Most frequent among these was 'Magnolia Jon', who had two small dogs of uncertain pedigree, which he bought into the bar each day after their exercise along the sea front.

Magnolia Jon was unusual amongst our group, in that he only ever drank coffee. Indeed, when Gloria Glendinning was still running the show, he was in the vanguard of those promoting the idea that The Smug should serve morning coffee, and possibly afternoon tea, in an attempt to draw in the tourists who still visited the town, perhaps in transit to our more popular neighbours up the coast.

There are several people called Jon or John amongst our little band of thinkers, and as a retired painter and decorator, 'Magnolia Jon' was identified by his nickname.

He liked the moniker and even had it painted on the side of his elderly faded van, which was a regular sight around the housing developments in the town as he worked, before he reached retirement age.

Now the van, which was originally red and owned by the Post Office and had faded to a sort of chalky pink, sat outside the little terraced house where he lived alone, still with his ladders padlocked to the roof rails, but rarely, if ever, used now. Jon, and the dogs of course, liked to walk everywhere and had no need to drive.

Fortunately the dogs were very well behaved, or possibly exhausted after their lengthy morning walk, and did not trouble Augustus, who usually took up station at the other end of the bar, while they were on the premises. Today, however, the dogs were asleep under their master's chair and Augustus felt that he could join us at the table.

'Yes, I see what you mean, Major,' Magnolia Jon said now. 'You could say The Smug is the cultural centre of the town, now that almost everything else has closed down. Other than in the old people's flats, it is about the only place where people can go to meet, and that.'

We all agreed with that in principle, but some pointed out to Jon that we preferred to describe Homely House as 'Retirement Apartments', rather than 'old people's flats', and that some of us were not really elderly or infirm enough to be called 'old people' quite yet.

The Major had done his research well, however, and the idea he floated now fascinated us all.

In an attempt to stop Local Authorities selling off playing fields, in particular, for housing developments, the Major had discovered details of a piece of legislation which became law during the time his late wife served on the Parish Council. The Major had been to the Library in the busy shopping centre a few miles away and obtained a photocopy of the details of the Act, which he read from now.

'If you will allow me' he said, 'I think this is the most relevant part ...' And, after clearing his throat he began to read.

"A building or other land is an asset of community value if its main use has recently been or is presently used to further the social wellbeing or social interests of the local community and could do so in the future. The Localism Act states that 'social interests' include cultural, recreational and sporting interests.

Assets of Community Value need to be registered with a Local Planning Authority by a voluntary or community body with a local connection (for example a Parish Council). Once listed, if an Asset of Community Value comes up for sale, the community have an opportunity to make a bid to purchase the asset. Initially there will be a period in which communities can express an intention to bid for an asset, this is followed by a period during which communities can prepare their bid. The owner cannot dispose of the asset during this time."

'But hang on, there is a complication,' said the Major, and continued to read.

"The owner is under no obligation to accept the bid – the provisions do not restrict who an owner can sell their property to or at what price and communities bidding have no right of first refusal."

For a moment we all sat in silence, and looking from face to face, the Major smiled, and avoiding the puddle of spilled beer, put his photocopy on the table, for anyone to see.

-oOo-

'We can't raise that sort of money ourselves!' exclaimed Biggles. 'This pub might be a bit grotty but it must be worth millions! Scraping up a few bob ta get the gas certificate so Mike and Emma can sell breakfasts, and that, is one thing, but buying the whole pub? Tha's impossible!'

'And,' said Gazza, 'how could we prove The Smug had been ... what was it? "Used to further the social wellbeing," and so-on "of the local community". This is just a pub where a bunch of old gits meet to sit about and talk about nothing much.'

'Well there,' said the Major, 'You may have put your finger on the precise issue the Act is there to promote ...'

'Eh?' said Magnolia Jon.

'There is nowhere else in the town for us to go,' added the Major. 'And what we regard as the route to our 'social wellbeing' comes out of the taps behind this very bar, and encourages the conversation and interactions we all engage in daily.'

'Wha's he say?' asked Biggles.

'But how would you even start such a thing?' asked Mike, collecting empty glasses from the table.

'We need a meeting with a Parish councillor,' declared the Major. 'And I know just the chap!'

-oOo-

The following morning, Barry Beeching turned up in his company car to meet an Estate Agent who would be measuring up and taking photographs.

Mike had been alerted to the visit, which was to take place before the pub opened, and he reluctantly let them in. Emma had taken herself off to the shops in the nearby town to keep herself busy and out of the way.

'Gawd blimey!' exclaimed the agent as he got out of his car. 'If I'm not mistaken, that is Japanese Knotweed, growing up that bit of scaffolding. That is going to cause us a problem!'

'Eh?' said Barry.

'Japanese Knotweed, mate. It has to be professionally removed. Killing it off can take as long as three years!'

'Well that would be a buyer's problem, wouldn't it? We would sell it 'as seen' surely. Let the buyer beware and all that stuff.'

'Well no, it doesn't quite work like that with Japanese Knotweed. I'm not an expert, but, if that is what I think it is, it can mean buyers can't get a mortgage on the place, and you have to tell them it is there by law.'

'Wouldn't it be the Council's responsibility to deal with it?'

'No, I'm afraid it is for the property owner to do it, and you have to take measures to stop it spreading to any adjacent land.'

'But …'

'You can still sell with the Knotweed there, but you have to tell prospective buyers, and I need to warn you it can knock the value right down.'

'How much?'

'Every case is different, of course, but there have been instances where it makes the property worthless, if nobody can get mortgages or commercial loans.'

'Is it dangerous?'

'Oh no, it is quite safe and won't do you or any pets any harm, but it has to be professionally treated to kill it off. You can't just cut it down and burn it, you have to get it poisoned and the roots removed or buried in deep sealed pits, when it is confirmed they are dead.'

'What would you suggest?'

'Well, I'll still measure up, as I'm here, but then it is over to you. Get the professionals in, mate, and call us back when you know what they have to say.'

Mike had listened carefully to this conversation. He wondered how this would affect the plans being brewed up in the bar.

-oOo-

Marlon Evans and his wife Anne had owned and run the fish and chip shop, next door to the amusement arcade, since they were in their early thirties.

As a child, Anne knew Marlon's family, who ran what was initially a jellied-eel shop on the fringes of the London Docklands and watched as it developed into a 'champagne and oyster bar' as the fortunes of the area improved over time.

As his parent's business became more successful Marlon was able to attend a catering college, and then, after a few years working in a fast food restaurant, with the help of a loan from his father, he was able to buy the fish and chip shop in what was then a bustling little seaside town.

Anne knew Marlon from school, and lived just down

the road from Marlon's parents. She was taken by her parents to their jellied-eel shop on high days and holidays and had accepted Marlon's proposal of marriage after just their second date, as soon as they were old enough.

They had been together now for almost thirty years, and apart from holidays, had never missed a day working side by side in the fish and chip shop.

They were both fat and contented, but were dealt an awful blow when a letter arrived from the County Council informing them that the sea front and some of the town was to be included in a Government regeneration scheme aimed at 'levelling up' deprived communities. This would involve the demolition of all the shops and buildings along the parade, road improvements, and the creation of a new 'community' of housing. It would, they said breathlessly, "create many new employment opportunities, during the building work and beyond, and produce affordable as well as open market housing for sale, to create a vibrant new seaside community for the town, which took advantage of its picturesque setting and natural amenities, whilst maximising its potential as a place to live."

The concept of the scheme was nothing new. It had been first discussed at a 'public consultation' in the early 1990's, but the idea was shelved when no funding was forthcoming. Now it emerged the Government had the funds to invest and had convinced a group of property developers to take it on. The Council had new Planning powers too, and could deal with any dissenting property owners by exercising their 'Compulsory Purchase' capabilities if necessary.

According to the artists impression, the amusement arcade and the fish and chip shop would disappear under a wide futuristic development of flats and expensive looking boutiques, which stretched as far as the old Seaview Guest House and swallowed up the former Lifeboat Inn.

Generally, Marlon and Anne did not drink, but they closed early that night and went to the pub to drown their sorrows.

-oOo-

CHAPTER 5

'And they have all got to be registered on the Electoral Roll here,' Timothy Fisher from the Parish Council was explaining. 'I looked up the rules when you told me why you wanted to meet.'

'Twenty one?' said Major Harris.

'At least twenty-one. More if you can get them. In fact the more signatories the better.'

'And do you think the Parish Council would be prepared to promote this scheme. Tim?'

'They might, but I think you are going to have to beef up the "presently used to further social wellbeing" bit of the requirements. I've been hearing about you giving English lessons to those Ukrainian refugees, by the way. Does that take place in the pub?'

'Er, would it help if it did?'

'It could well be helpful. There is a lot of concern in Local Government circles to be seen to be doing all we can to help these poor blighters at the moment.'

'Does a pub need permission to do that sort of thing?'

'I don't think so, so long as the building owners don't object, and it doesn't breach the alcohol licence, of course.'

'Oh no, the lessons don't take place when the pubs are open.'

'But they do take place in this pub, and you will be able to demonstrate that?'

'I will have that all sorted out by the time we fill in the forms, Tim,' replied the Major.

He would have to go down to the Seaview Guest House as soon as this meeting finished, and tell his friends there that the venue for their English lessons had changed, and they would now be meeting in The Smug.

-o0o-

'Surely they can't just chuck you out,' said Emma, later that evening. 'You must have a lease on the shop, haven't you?'

'Well, yes, we have,' said Anne, 'but the Council have what they call "Compulsory Purchase powers" so we can't stop them buying us out.'

'There is no firm timescale on all this yet,' said Marlon, putting down his empty glass on the bar. 'They are talking about two years, but who really knows.'

'Another one?' asked Emma, reaching for the glass.

'I think we have had enough, don't you, Marlon?' said Anne.

'No. Same again please Emma,' grumbled Marlon. 'I have not had nearly enough yet.'

-oOo-

'We had tha' Jap Weed on they school playing fields, up near the railway embankment,' explained Biggles. 'They had to get these specialist blokes in, like.'

'You don't happen to remember who they were, do you Biggles?' asked Mike, pouring another pint of bitter.

'Nah, but I could ask Mrs Brown, the school Secretary. She an' me stay in touch, see. She says she wants to see if I'm managing, but really I know it's 'cos she fancies me.'

-oOo-

The following morning the usual crew were in. We of the Smug were intrigued by what the Major had to say and anxious to hear how his meeting with his contact at the Parish Council went.

'There was a pub just like this in Peckham, wot we done,' Gazza was saying, while we waited for the Major to arrive. 'It ain't been messed abaht like this one, but the building started off more or less the same layout.'

'What big and draughty, you mean?' said Magnolia Jon.

'Nah, I mean it was like it was when it was built. Three sep'rit bars.'

'How's that work then?'

'Well, the people wanted it left as it was designed. Retro style, like. It had a Public bar for the proleetare... for the prelate... for the common folk; a posher Lounge Bar, for the toffs, and a little Snug for ... well, I dunno what for really. But it all felt much more cozy than this.'

'And your firm got the job of doing it up, did they?' asked Mike as he passed by.

'Well, it was Susie, my missus, what got us the restoration work. I told you she worked for an Architectural Technician, didn't I. Drawing up the plans like.'

'I think you mentioned it once or twice,' said Magnolia Jon, rolling his eyes.

'That sounds interesting,' said Mike. 'Is she very artistic?'

'Artistic? Well, I dunno about that, but she was working as a draughtsman, or draughts-person perhaps we should say nah. Did dead complicated technical plans she did. Electrical layouts and everything.'

'And you worked as a builder doing shop fit-outs and that sort of thing?'

'Tha's right, Mike. I'm a carpenter by trade, see, and me an' Susie helped each other out when we could, like.'

'If you are not careful, Mike,' said Jon, 'Gazza here will demonstrate how sharp his memory is, even today, by explaining all the details of every job he has ever worked on, right back to when God was in short trousers.'

'You can go off people, you know Jon ...' said Gazza.

'Not when they are buying you another lager, though,' chuckled Magnolia Jon.

-oOo-

CHAPTER 6

When Major Harris arrived, we of The Smug clustered round, anxious to hear what he had to say.

He started by handing round further photocopies of the information about the 'Localism Act' we had discussed before, and then explained what was involved if we were to take a 'bid' forward.

'I dun even know twenty-one people, let alone whether they are on this voter's list thing,' said Biggles with a look of dismay in his one eye.

'But think how many people live up Homely House,' said Magnolia Jon helpfully. 'I bet we could get nearly enough signatures up there on its own, if we tried.'

'Good point,' said the Major. 'But we are going to have to get as many signatures as we can, not just the initial twenty-one, apparently.'

'We could do a leaflet drop, and put up posters, and that,' said Gazza.

'An excellent idea, and I'm sure young Jake at Speedy Press who made these copies for me would be prepared to help with that,' smiled the Major. 'But there is a much more important point we have to address first.'

'Go on,' said Emma.

'If we manage to convince the Parish Council to allow us to register this place as a "Asset of Community Value" it means we have six months to refine our proposals during which the brewery are not allowed to sell it. But we have got to think about where the money is coming from. And if we do this we need to be able to prove that we can raise the finance.'

'So they won't be able to sell for six months when we register this thing?' asked Mike.

'Correct, although don't lose sight of the fact that the brewery don't have to sell it to us. They can sell to whoever they like.'

'Yes but that gives us, Emma and me, six months more to live here. That is enough time for us to make some money out of this breakfast idea, that might help a bit.'

'Every little will help, Mike, and it will be a start,' said the Major. 'It will also show that the business at the pub can grow with new ideas, and that might help our business case if we need to borrow money.'

'We could get this Jake bloke to print some leaflets up about the breakfasts,' said Gazza. 'And we could divide the district up into chunks and each go and deliver some, door to door, like.'

'Another great idea!' said the Major.

'And Mike and I will pay for the printing as our contribution,' said Emma.

Just then the door opened and in walked Marlon from the chip shop.

'Hair of the dog please, Mike,' he said.

-oOo-

Fortunately their previous pub was insured, but the time it was taking to get the insurance company to pay their claim seemed to be stretching on interminably.

Mike and Emma had watched their hopes and dreams literally go up in smoke, and Emma was quite badly injured in the fire, but all the insurance company wanted to do was quibble over details. Was Emma's grandmother's rocking chair really victorian and had they got any paperwork about it … Could Mike prove that he had paid for the carpets fitted a year before the fire … When was the wiring last checked … Could the Fire Service confirm the exact time they were called out … And so it went on.

Recently the irritating flow of questions seemed to

have dried up, and Mike and Emma took that as a hopeful sign. Over the past few weeks it had seemed that each time they dealt with one issue, they were notified of another. Granted the insurance company had made a payment towards the cost of their temporary accommodation and a much smaller payment to cover 'subsistence', but the rest seemed to be in a blizzard of paperwork which they had to wade through on an almost daily basis.

While all this was going on however, Mike and Emma still had to keep paying their mortgage each month. The bank which provided the funds was aware of the problem but, while they were very sorry, they pointed out that the terms of the commercial loan were clear. It was not like a domestic mortgage where one might be able to negotiate a 'payment holiday' in similar circumstances, and until it was paid off completely, each month a payment had to be made.

Then there was the car loan, which still had a year to go …

Emma shuddered as she remembered the awful night of the fire. It still haunted her dreams. For a while she had regularly woken up screaming, and found it difficult to calm down until Mike wrapped her tightly in his arms and almost shouted at her that it was all right, and that she was safe now.

The worst part of her recurring dream was when she found herself looking back at the pub as she was running away from it, and saw a section of the thatched roof, well alight, sliding to the ground. That was the moment she realised that Augustus, their cat, might still be inside, and she pulled herself free from whoever it was that was trying to drag her away from the conflagration, and started to run back.

In this awful dream, her legs were somehow immensely heavy and would not run as she wanted and desperately needed them to do. That was when she heard it.
The unmistakable cry of her beloved cat. And it was coming from inside the building.

-oOo-

Before the fire, their pub had become quite successful, and they were starting to reap the rewards of ten years of hard work. They had employed staff and could afford holidays, but now, with only the wages from their 'temporary' job at The Smug to support them, Mike and Emma were getting into debt.

Emma in particular felt very sorry for the staff they had taken on, who over the years had become friends rather than just employees. Two of the five were still out of work and she kept in touch with them all on a daily basis with mobile phone messages. She would employ them all again in a heartbeat, if she had something to offer them.

Mike was becoming increasingly frustrated. He was the 'ideas man' of the team, and continually came up with ways to improve the experience for their customers, and enhance their business. But working for the brewery was constraining. Other than the breakfast idea, he had not been able to make any changes or improvements at The Smug, although he could see several areas that could be made much more profitable and efficient, if only he had the chance.

Only Augustus, the cat, was happy with his new life, and for him things were about to get even better.

-oOo-

'Well,' said Marlon, 'that's it for the repairs. I'm not doing them now.'

'Repairs?' said Mike.

'Yes. The shop has a flat roof bit at the back which is parting company from the main structure. We have a 'full repairing and insuring lease' and the Landlord is insisting we pay to get it rebuilt.'

'That sounds expensive.'

'It might be, but that is not all. One of the fryers is up the spout and needs changing and there is a broken window on the toilet round the back,' Marlon took another sip of his beer. 'Now that I've had time to take in this 'regeneration scheme' properly and think about it a bit, I'm coming to the conclusion that we might actually do better just to give up and move somewhere else.'

'But I thought the chip shop was always busy?' said

Mike.

'Oh it is. Quite a goldmine, if I'm honest. Anne and I don't go out much ... we don't have time ... so we have saved up a nice little pile of money in recent years, and with no kids we don't have any debt. I'm thinking we might sell our bungalow and retire.'

'Is that what you want?'

'No, to be honest Mike, I would hate it. I've always loved the shop and being busy and so on, and so has Anne. I know we will have to retire one day, but there is plenty of life left in us yet ...'

'How long has your lease got to run on the shop, Marlon?'

'Er, about three years. Why?'

'Oh, just an idea,' said Mike. 'Another beer?'

-oOo-

The meeting back at the brewery had gone well until Barry Beeching had to tell his boss about the Japanese Knotweed at The Smug.

Roy Sommers, the Area Finance Director (Designate), responsible for the group of properties, which included The Smug, was a nasty spiteful little man who had said several times in Board meetings that he did not see why they needed to continue to employ three 'Acquisitions Managers' when they were not looking to acquire any new properties, and were anxious to dispose of some of those they already had on the books.

He was fiercely ambitious and had his eye firmly fixed on the Managing Director's job, if the charming but ineffectual last member of the original family at the brewery that bore his name, put a foot wrong.

Barry knew that nobody liked the angry little accountant, who bullied his staff, but unfortunately he was rather good at his job, so he represented a serious threat.

When Barry explained about the Japanese Knotweed, the accountant seethed with impotent rage and interrupted with snide comments as Barry went through the process and the timescale for dealing with the problem. Eventually the Managing Director intervened and pointed out that the appearance of the problem of an invasive weed could not be blamed on Barry, but that, with his long experience of dealing with the properties on the brewery's estate, they should be confident that Barry was the man to deal with it properly.

As the meeting ended, Sommers was heard to mutter that the easy solution would be to burn the ruddy pub down and deal with it that way.

-oOo-

Marlon was about to leave when the Ukrainian mothers and children started to turn up at the pub.

Marlon had a conversation in the carpark in which, among other things, he told Major Harris that the little girl called Ivanna always cuddled Augustus when they met outside the fish and chip shop, on a Friday. Augustus gave a chirrup of joy as he saw the group arriving for their first English lesson in the pub.

-oOo-

CHAPTER 7

Timothy Fisher from the Parish Council had taken an interest in what we of The Smug were attempting to do.

He had taken the time to go through the idea with the other Councillors, some of whom where initially sceptical, but at least said they would listen to any proposal the group wanted to make when the time came.

Major Harris, meanwhile, had been looking into what was involved in the formation of an 'Industrial and Provident Society'; a sort of company used by registered charities, and essential if the proposal to create a "Community Asset" was to succeed. At that point he realised that perhaps some legal advice was needed.

'Thanks for arranging this, Tim,' he said; as we all shook hands with Arthur Glenn, the former Borough Solicitor, who had managed just six months of blissfully peaceful retirement before he had been asked to lend a hand, and for no fee, mind you, to advise us.

In the meeting that followed, it was revealed that it was possible to raise capital by issuing shares, and that it was necessary to set up an Industrial and Provident Society to be able to abide by the rules which govern co-operative societies.

Arthur explained that these shares, known as 'Community Shares', would enable residents to invest financially in a community project, by buying shares and becoming part-owners of a business. He said that local people could become supporters, volunteers and advocates, not just customers, and projects would get much needed funding to get started and become financially sustainable.

In the recent past, Arthur pointed out, this method had been used to run community farms, establish community shops or purchase solar panels, and interestingly not all the funding for the project needed to be raised through shares. It was possible that once we had this as a base, it could attract larger private investors too.

There was some discussion about the pricing of shares and the methodology of setting up the process, as well as how to get people to commit to it.

'But first,' said Tim, 'You need to agree what it is you are trying to do in a sentence or two, and get those twenty-one or more people to sign up to a form of words, which we can help you with, so that you can start the process of registering your Community Asset.'

It was all getting rather exciting.

'How do Emma and I go about getting on the local Electoral Role here, so we can join in?' asked Mike.

-oOo-

'Magnolia Jon' closed his front door having said goodbye to the Tesco delivery man.

Since Covid he had continued to shop on line and have his groceries delivered. It was so much easier. The same order every month worked well for him, although he did add occasional treats if he fancied something different every now and then.

Unfortunately, today the delivery was late, and he was going to have to hurry to get up to The Smug in time for the start of the meeting they were having there. But progress was slowed once again when his mobile phone rang.

It was David, his son.

'Yes,' he said, 'that will be no problem. My mate Kev is a qualified gas engineer, as I thought, and he has the right registrations, and that, to work on a commercial oven and issue a safety ticket.'

'Excellent!' said Jon.

'Better hurry up and book him for this pub job though,

Dad. He's is off on holiday to his villa in Spain for three weeks soon.'

'He has a villa in Spain?'

'Of course he does, Dad. He's a plumber!'

-oOo-

'Sorry to call so early,' said Eric, when Mike opened the door at eight that morning. 'Gazza said you needed an electrician to safety certify the kitchen equipment, so you can do breakfasts here, and I was passing on my way to work.'

'Right ...' said Mike shaking the water from the shower out of his ears.

'No charge, of course, if it means I can come and have breakfast here on my way to work when you get it up and running.'

'Well,' smiled Mike. 'You had better come in!'

-oOo-

'What the hell is this all about?' snarled Roy Sommers. 'How can they stop us selling for six months. It is our property!'

'It is because of the 'Localism Act' which came into force a few years ago. People can apply to register something as a "Community Asset" if they can get enough support and ...'

'Ridiculous!' screeched Sommers. 'Make them stop! Do

something about it!'

'Well, I'm not sure what we ...'

'This would happen now, wouldn't it, what with the Year End ...'

'How does that ...'

'The Year End, Barry! Bonuses! Our region is so close to reaching our target. If we get this damn pub sold, or even get a ten-percent deposit on exchange of contracts in time, we could make it. But we are running out of other options and it is too late to get anything else sold off.'

'But ...'

'But, Barry, if you don't get that grubby old dump sold in time I, I mean we, don't get our bonuses this year! Nothing! Nothing at all!'

'I ...'

'I don't care how you do it, or what you have to do, just get those idiots to stop this, and get that ruddy pub in the auction and sold!'

'But the Japanese Knotweed ...'

'Never mind about that. Tell the auctioneer to put it in the details, but get it sold at any damn price! The Year End, Barry; The YEAR BLOODY END!'

-oOo-

Some children just seem to have an ear for these things.

Little Ivanna, sitting now on one of the bench seats under the window with Augustus on her lap was offering quite complicated responses to the gentle questions Major Harris posed in English.

She was much better than anyone else in the 'class', and was soon offering to help both adults and children who were struggling.

'Now maybe is good we coming speak the English only, Major. Yes, no?' she asked.

-oOo-

CHAPTER 8

It was debatable whether Barry Beeching should have gone anywhere near us in the light of events, but as he climbed out of his company car and came through the double doors, he asked we of The Smug where he might find a Major Peter Harris.

'That's me,' said The Major rising to his feet. 'Anything I can do for you?'

Barry explained who he was, and asked if there was somewhere they could speak in private. Mike offered his sitting room on the first floor.

The sitting room was crowded and untidy because Gloria Glendinning's possessions were still in place. Indeed it was she who had consented to Mike and Anne moving into the living accommodation over the bar, when we of The Smug explained their plight. Officially she was still the tenant.

Perching uncomfortably on the edge of a tired sofa, Barry Beeching gave a little cough and thanked the

Major for seeing him. He had said very little more before the Major raised a hand and said that, now that he understood what this was about, he wanted to ask a few other people to join the meeting.

We of The Smug squeezed into the little sitting room where we could, and Barry Beeching began again.

The last straw for Barry was not so much when he was told that someone in the Parish Council had been discussing a bid to declare the place as a 'Community Asset', but that he should get that news from that odious little bully, Roy Sommers.

If he had found out about it in any other way he might have reacted differently. But the fact that that little creep should get one over on him by telling him what was going on in his area of the business, and then the way he gloated about it, was what really rankled.

Now he had to get the inside story, directly from those involved, to get ahead of the game.

Major Harris told him in a straightforward and honest way about our plans, and apart from expressing regret that we had not been able to inform the brewery ourselves, he kept nothing back.

'I am rather disappointed that you should hear about it from someone at the Parish Council who should not have been talking about it, following what was, after all, a confidential consultation, but at least you now have the full facts, Mr Beeching.'

'Thank you for being so candid, Major … and please call me Barry, I am not your enemy here, and may even be able to help you.'

'You can help us?' asked the Major. And then Barry Beeching did something none of us expected, and that would certainly have got him sacked from his job, if it got out. He told us all about the views of Roy Sommers, in his office, and gave us an almost verbatim account of his last conversation with him.

-oOo-

The letter from the Estate Agent was waiting for Barry when he got to his desk, and he read it with interest, and some dismay, before he even poured himself a mug of coffee.

The agent confirmed what he had said when he visited the pub, particularly about the damage to the value and saleability that the presence of Japanese Knotweed would mean.

The letter ended with the comment that the brewery might be well advised to resolve the Knotweed issue before they considered putting it up for sale.

The agent's valuation in the letter was also a disappointment, but less of a surprise, given the run-down state the area the pub was in, and how under used it had become.

In the letter, the agent assumed the pub would be

closed and boarded up by the time it was offered for sale by auction, and suggested that they could advertise ahead of the auction to attract suggestions for alternative uses of the site and buildings, perhaps for redevelopment, to try to maximise the value.

Barry made copies for the Managing Director and for Roy Sommers, the accountant, and prepared to deliver them.

-o0o-

Generally Barry Beeching led a quiet life.

Since, in the tenth year of their marriage, one day before their anniversary, when his wife had left him and moved in with a tall dashing man from her firm's finance department in the newspaper office where she worked, Barry had a deep dislike of accountants. He categorised them along with estate agents and life insurance salesmen as the least trustworthy of men.

The dashing accountant in question was eight years younger than his wife, and Barry had actually met him at her company's Christmas 'do'. He could not help noticing how she fluttered round him like some silly schoolgirl, and he played up to her as the interminable festive event dragged on.

Afterwards, in the car on the way home, he asked her about it. She said not to be silly, of course, but six weeks later she had packed her bags and gone.

Fortunately Barry had his work. He was good at it and

diligent, and enjoyed what he did very much.

If it wasn't for the bullying tactics and wheedling snide comments Roy Sommers threw at him whenever the Managing Director wasn't looking, Barry would have been quite content.

He found he had no strong desire to find female company, although he did briefly try one of those 'on-line' dating sites. But he found it nearly as uncomfortable, artificial, and somehow grubby as the amateur dramatics his wife had tried to involve him in some years before.

He found solace in his passion for his collection of model trains, and finding rare rolling stock for the track layout he had built up over several years in the loft of his semi-detached house.

He built scale models of railway stations and even had a section of the London Underground built into the diorama he created, all of which could be controlled from a complicated hand built dashboard.

Nobody had ever seen the system he had built, but that was just the way he liked it. He felt no need to show it off, and had no desire to share it with anyone.

-oOo-

'Thank you for letting me think about it overnight, Barry,' said the Major into his mobile phone. 'I have a proposition for you.'

'Go on,' said Barry, sitting in his company car, in traffic.

'I noted what you said about being under pressure to put the property in to the earliest available auction to get it sold, even if it meant taking a loss, or at least not maximising its full potential.'

'I said all that in the strictest confidence …'

'Yes, yes. You made that abundantly clear, but this conversation is also confidential and very much just between the two of us.'

'OK? …'

'So, given those conditions, my proposition is unofficial at present but before I make it a firm offer, I would like your view as to whether it might be possible.'

'Right, well just between us, then, what have you in mind?'

'I'll come straight to the point. Look Barry, you and I both know that, as a going concern, if trading conditions were good, the pub might be worth as much as say three-hundred thousand, or maybe a bit more. That is, if it were not for three things. There is the Japanese Knotweed, the parlous state of the finances, and our bid for "Community Asset" status, which could sterilise the potential for a sale for six months or more. But if you close it down, board it up and put it in an auction sale with those constraints against it, it won't make anything like that, and may not even sell at all.'

'And your point is?'

'You have been very candid with us about the pressure on you to get the money you need in your bank in time for your 'year end', and if you would consider a straight forward cash sale of the place as it is, ahead of any auction, with full disclosure of the Japanese Knotweed and so-on taken as read, I might be prepared to make you an offer.'

'You?'

'Yes, not the group. The offer would be from me personally. Although I have to say that the 'Community Asset' application will still proceed once the transaction has gone through and the ultimate aim would be that the group end up owning it.'

'Well, this is a surprise ...'

'There are a couple of conditions, however. My offer would be to exchange contracts with a ten-percent deposit, paid as soon as the lawyers could do the paperwork, but to delay completion for six-months from the date of exchange.'

'I see. You said a couple of conditions ...'

'Yes. The second is that the brewery will agree to support the 'Community Asset' bid and raise no objection to it being promoted.'

'Anything else?'

'Well the last point is actually in favour of the brewery, a sweetener if you like. I would like to enter into an arrangement where the brewery continue to provide wines, beer and spirits, as before, on commercial terms, for at least twelve months, and that you will support an application for my nominee to become the landlord, and hold the licence of the establishment, when the deal is done.'

'Phew. That's a lot to take in. But more importantly, how much are you prepared to offer, and if you don't mind me asking, have you got the money?'

The Major chucked at that.

'Have no concerns about the money, Barry. My solicitor will be prepared to confirm that the funds are available.'

'And the price?'

'Do you think your company would consider an offer of one hundred and fifty thousand?'

-oOo-

'I got it!' said Biggles. 'I got the number of them Knotweed people what got rid of it at the school.'

'Well done Biggles,' said Magnolia Jon.

'Yus. Mrs Brown dug it aht for me. An' she told me

what they had to do, too. First off they has to do a survey, see.'

'I see,' said Gazza. 'Makes sense, that does.'

'But it ain't free. We 'av to pay for them to come.'

'Any idea how much?'

'Well, I didn't actually ask ... I thought the Major, or one of you could ...'

'Yes, all right Biggles. We will take it from here,' said Magnolia Jon. 'What is the number?'

-oOo-

'They are called The Grounds Management Group PLC,' said the Major. 'And the chap there said they want two hundred pounds to come out and have a look at it and tell us what they have to do to get rid of it.'

'Two hundred pounds just to give us a quote? Blimey!' said Gazza. 'If I could've charged for quotes back in the day, I could just have lived on that. I'd never actually have had to do any work!'

'You never did much work anyway,' said Susie, who usually stayed at home during the week, but had joined us for a look around the pub, at Mike and Emma's request, given the progress we were making.

'See, that's why I married her,' smiled Gazza. 'Always so supportive.'

'We could have a whip round …' said Magnolia Jon.

So we did.

-oOo-

CHAPTER 9

'You must be joking!' snarled Roy Sommers. 'Tell him he has got to try harder than that if he wants us to do an "off-the-market" deal with him, Barry. We do have to get it past the shareholders, you know.'

'Well, now Roy,' said the Managing Director, 'you know, given all the problems, a sale for cash ...'

'Yes, but the Estate Agent said it might be worth about two-hundred if we could sort out the Knotweed first. This bloke is wanting fifty grand off!'

'But from my reading around the matter, Roy, the fact that Japanese Knotweed might once have been present can blight a property, and make it un-mortgageable, even if it has been removed,' said the Managing Director. 'We might not be able to sell it at all.'

'Are you saying we should take the offer, sir?' asked Barry.

'I think it would be wise if you were to use your well

known powers of persuasion, Barry, and see if you can get him to come up a little,' said the Managing Director. 'And bring back what I believe is called his "best and final offer", and then we will see.'

'Do you want me to take this over and push this bloke, rather than just leave it to Barry?'

'No thank you, Roy. Barry is very experienced in this sort of negotiation, and is, after all, our property expert. See what you can do, Barry, and report back directly to me would you?'

In the corridor, as they left the meeting room, Roy hissed 'Just get the bloody deal done and get the lawyers moving on it, Barry. We don't have long. Speed is everything!'

-oOo-

'I think it could work really well, Anne,' said Marlon. 'And we will be buying it, remember, not just renting it on a one sided shop lease, so no rent rises, or arguments about repairs, ever again.'

'Well, it does seem a great idea, Marlon, but do you know how much it is going to cost.'

'Not yet, sweetheart. There's equipment and fittings to be priced up and that sort of thing. But it could be just the lucky break we need, and you know we have got enough money saved in the bank, if it works out.'

'It might …' said Anne.

'And I shall so enjoy telling the landlord to stick his "full repairing and insuring lease" right up ...'

'Marlon! There are ladies present.'

'Only you, my lovely lady, and we are going to make our future much more certain, if this comes off!'

-oOo-

In his company car, on the way to discuss the offer with the Major, Barry took a call from Sir Jeremy Beauchamp, who for many years had been the brewery's trusted corporate lawyer.

'Good morning, Sir Jeremy,' said Barry.

'Good morning, dear boy. I'm glad I caught you. Can you talk?'

'I'm driving but the call is hands-free, so yes.'

'And you are on your own?'

'Yes, Sir Jeremy ... is everything all right?'

'Well, I think so. But I thought I ought to let you know that I have had a most odd call from Roy Sommers in your office, and he offered to double my fee if I got contracts exchanged on the sale of a certain premises before the twenty-third of next month.'

-oOo-

'And who is Roy Sommers again, Barry?' asked the Major, as they sat in the empty bar of The Smug.

'The Area Finance Director at the brewery, and a self serving, self-important, little so-and-so.'

'He certainly isn't what you would call charming,' said Mike. 'Emma and I met him briefly when we were offered this place. You would think he was doing us a huge favour by offering us work here, when in reality the opposite was true. He was desperate for someone to open the pub that very day, after the previous Temporary Managers did a moonlight flit. We were appointed because we could step in immediately, and were prepared to sort out the problems here. He told us that although he was very busy, he would be in to help us settle in soon, but we haven't heard any more from him since.'

'Well, I suppose there are reasons for his aggressive behaviour,' said Barry. 'He has four teenage daughters, who are all into ponies and designer clothes, by his first wife, and his second wife has just announced that she is pregnant.'

'He *is* a busy little chap, then,' chuckled the Major.

'And he makes no secret of the fact that he is after the Managing Director's job when the old boy finally conks out, and is prepared to cut any corners, short of actual murder, to get there.'

'I see,' smiled the Major. 'Ah, the first of my English students are starting to arrive. Will you let them in, please Mike ...'

'So what can I report back, Major,' asked Barry, preparing to leave.

'Tell them I will raise my offer by another five thousand, but if that is not accepted by this time tomorrow I will withdraw altogether. That ought to put the willies up your nasty Mr Sommers!'

-oOo-

'They will be here on Tuesday,' said Magnolia Jon. 'The survey doesn't take long, apparently, and they will be able to work out what to do and might be able to give us an idea of price there and then.'

'Good. I don't like the idea of living with an invasive weed growing up outside my bedroom window,' said Emma. 'I've read The Day of the Triffids, you know!'

-oOo-

'I get it. That will work well, Susie' said Gazza, studying the plans she had drawn, later that afternoon.

'And I can't see the Planners objecting because there was something similar there originally.'

'I've been chatting to the boys in the betting shop next door,' Gazza announced, 'and they are all for it. They also want us to let them know when they can buy these shares, if we go down that route, and will sign our petition, or whatever its called to help us get the twenty-one names.'

'But there is still the problem of how we are going to raise the money quick enough to stop the brewery selling it to someone else,' said Magnolia Jon. 'We might get promises - 'pledges' Arthur, the lawyer, called them, but my David ran a half marathon for charity once, and it took him months to get the money out of those who promised to sponsor him.'

'Well, I might have some news on that front,' said the Major, returning his mobile phone to his pocket as he re-joined our little group.

-o0o-

If we of The Smug could have carried the Major shoulder high through the town to thank him for his heroism, it would still not have been enough.

His generosity, both of spirit, commitment, and indeed in terms of risking hard cash, had astonished us all. And his cleverness in sorting out this deal to save The Smug as an 'Asset of Community Value' took our breath away.

Arthur, the former Borough Solicitor, dragged himself out of the longed for retirement he had only just started to enjoy, and worked night and day. He became a consultant, alongside and under the banner of the Major's own well established London lawyers. Together they were working towards getting the deal through in time, and in a form that encompassed our 'Community Asset' aspirations. It would be quite an achievement when it was done.

Meanwhile, signatures were being added to the 'pledge forms' for prospective stakeholders, and a new 'Industrial and Provident Society' with charitable status was set up and incorporated as a 'Co-operative and Community Benefit Society', to create the business plan for our new venture and enable us to sell shares. It was complicated, but Arthur found and introduced us to a voluntary organisation with experience in these matters who agreed to help and advise us. Fortunately they had done it before and their advice, when they came to see us, was invaluable.

As the number of signatures passed sixty-five, the Parish Council formally agreed to support the proposal and the process of registering The Smug as an 'Asset of Community Value' began.

There was hectic activity for we of The Smug as well, as we were involved in delivering leaflets all around the district about Mike and Emma's breakfasts being served, and then about the plans for taking over the pub on behalf of the community.

It was as the breakfast was being served, and after we had delivered the second set of leaflets that Mike and Emma had a visitor.

'Hello,' he said. 'Are you in charge here? I'm Darren Spiro from Wideacre Developments. Can we have a chat about your proposals and our Government backed scheme to regenerate the sea-front area?'

-oOo-

'I've never met so many people in suits before in my life,' Marlon was saying. 'And I've never had to deal with so much paperwork, and that. It is exhausting!'

'But it is all coming together, Marlon,' said Susie, smiling. 'And our meeting with the Planning Officer yesterday about my drawings for the subdivision and reconfiguring the space was really positive …'

'Sorry to interrupt,' said Emma. 'But the letter and report from the Japanese Knotweed people has just come in the post and I think we need to discuss it.'

-oOo-

CHAPTER 10

Grounds Management Group PLC kept a low profile, and their surveyor arrived in an unmarked van.

'I think the bloke they sent out would have been happier to do his survey at the dead of night, given what he said about causing fear and upset in local neighbourhoods,' said Emma. 'He was an odd little man and was dressed in full camouflage kit, believe it or not. I think he fancied himself as a member of the SAS or something. He kept dodging about, didn't make eye contact and kept looking over his shoulder all the time he was here.'

When we of The Smug had finished chuckling at that, Emma read out the report.

There were several different methods they could employ to remove the Japanese Knotweed, they said, but the most complete, which seemed appropriate, given the need to retain public access to the property, was going to cost just shy of five-thousand pounds.

'And we can't just cut it dahn and burn it?' asked Gazza, going back over old ground.

Emma sighed, leafed back through the lengthy document which accompanied the letter, and read out the section on the rules for the removal of the invasive weed once again.

-oOo-

'So, these are the plans and the photocopies of the artists impressions he left,' Mike was saying, as he spread out the papers on the bar. 'They don't have full planning permission yet, but he said their application is going in next week.'

'And there will be a public consultation about such a major scheme, I should think,' said Susie.

'There will, Susie.' Mike tapped one of the pages on the bar. 'This is the timescale for it all to happen. Wideacre Developments have obviously been planning this for some time.'

'And they are prepared to support our own scheme?' said the Major.

'So this Mr Spiro said. It seems their original proposal for the sea-front redevelopment included a pub because the Planners thought they should put one into the commercial centre, as you see here,' Mike tapped the "artist's impression" page on the bar. 'But he said pubs are a liability in a scheme like this, and with so many going bust on a weekly basis they would be happy to design it out. If The Smug is going to stay, and he can say so in his application, it will mean they can put in another couple of boutiques or make the gym they plan a bit bigger. The Smug is only just down the road from it, after all.'

'Will the Planners go with that?' asked Magnolia Jon.

'Where are all the food places going ta be, then?' interrupted Biggles. 'If the chippy and the Indian goes, I'll starve!'

'Time to reveal the plans you have been working on with Marlon, I think, Susie,' said the Major.

-oOo-

'When it was built in 1925, this pub was called The Coach and Horses, and it was built in a plan form and style that was common at the time known as "Brewers Tudor",' began Susie. 'Suburban and provincial town public houses often had two or three bars and somewhere for 'off-sales', like an off-licence if you like, where people could buy unopened bottles of booze, without coming into the bar, to take it home.'

Gazza helped to unroll the plan she now laid out on the bar.

'Top left on this drawing, I've put what the original pub looked like and my best guess at the layout it had then. You will see there was a biggish public bar, to the left over towards the carpark. That beam over our heads now would have been where the wall was, dividing it from a much smaller room which might have be a "snug" or a billiard room, which was served through a hatch and used for more private get togethers, or to provide entertaining distractions for the drinkers.' Susie used a paper straw to point at the room in question. 'To the right of that was the lounge bar. The posher bar, where it might be acceptable to take a lady back then. And then the most interesting bit of all, from your point of view, Biggles …'

'Ay? said Biggles, almost, but not quite, spilling the glass of milk he always had with his breakfast.

'Between the lounge bar and the betting shop next door, there was the "off-sales" room. It was really a sort of shop with a window and a door to the street front and a counter accessed from inside where the publican could sell bottles of beer or spirits and so on.'

'What has that got to do with me?' asked Biggles.

'Because in the new proposal, that, along with a chunk of what was originally the lounge bar, will become Marlon and Anne's fish and chip shop!'

'Marlon, and Anne's …' Biggles struggled for a moment with the concept. 'You mean …'

'The chippy gets swallowed up in this new sea-front development,' explained Gazza. 'But we are going to incorporate a new and better chippy here, for Marlon and Anne to continue to trade.'

'It will help us make the case for this being a facility which continues to serve the community, as well as making our business plan more viable,' said the Major. 'Marlon and Anne have agreed, in principle, to buy what then becomes a separate shop, and trade alongside the pub, providing fish and chips for the punters in here too.'

'Blimey,' said Biggles. 'That's dead clever that is! I like it.'

'Glad you approve,' smiled Susie. 'Let's just hope the Planners like it too.'

-oOo-

Having visited The Smug to catch up on progress, Timothy Fisher from the Parish Council had taken a photocopy of the letter from the Japanese Knotweed removal company, and after consulting on it, telephoned Major Harris.

'It might be possible for the Parish Council to help with the Knotweed removal because it forms part of the 'Asset of Community Value' application. The scheme may be eligible for a Public Works Loan finance scheme, which the Parish can apply for, and in turn, can be passed on to your organisation as a grant. A 'PWL' is an affordable public loan which can be made to local councils for exactly this type of initiative.'

'That is wonderful news, Tim!' said the Major. 'What do we need to do to help you to get it for us?'

-oOo-

CHAPTER 11

'It was a heart attack, they said,' Sir Jeremy Beauchamp was speaking to Barry Beeching who took the call on his mobile phone, in his car, on his way in to work. Sir Jeremy was explaining that the Managing Director had been admitted to hospital overnight. 'His wife called me in the early hours.'

'Oh that is terrible …'

'They say it was a mild one, but at our age …'

'Is he the same age as you, Sir Jeremy?'

'I'm three years older. Did you know we were in the Navy together? I was his commanding officer at one point.'

'How is his wife taking it?'

'Well, she seems all right. She is at the hospital now, of course, and she sent me an email just now on his behalf, asking me to tell the people in the office, and to instruct the Area Finance Officers to sign any paperwork in his absence which needs urgent attention.'

Barry sighed. That was more bad news.

There were three Area Finance Officers in the company, the most senior of which was Roy Sommers, who was always anxious to tell anybody who would listen that his job title was Area Finance *Director* (Designate).

According to those who knew, in the HR department, the '(Designate)' was code for not quite appointed to the job yet. Apparently it was like being on a trial period before the promotion to become a Director was made final. Not that Roy Sommers looked at it that way, and he strutted about the office issuing instructions left, right, and centre, as if he owned the place, when the Managing Director wasn't looking.

'Oh dear. Roy Sommers is going to be unbearable when he hears that news,' said Barry.

-o0o-

Gloria Glendinning would have been in the same hospital as the Managing Director, but she had recently been moved to a special unit, off site, which offered a range of services. These including 'respite care', long term care services for visiting non-residential patients, such as chiropody, physiotherapy, and social activities for older persons. They also had beds for people who didn't need full hospital care, but for one reason or another could not be discharged completely.

Gloria was the only one suffering from what was being referred to as 'long covid', and as the symptoms seemed to be different in every case, the doctors and hospital administrators were at a loss as to what to do with her.

She had a daughter who lived in Leeds and visited very occasionally, but before her illness, she lived alone at the pub where she had been the tenant for many years, initially with her husband, and for the past twelve years on her own. The hospital couldn't simply turf her out, because she was still in no condition to look after herself, let alone go back to work running a pub.

Benedict Place had been set up as a public/private partnership with a housing charity to deal with just this sort of difficult situation for NHS patients. Gloria was happy enough there for now, but public funding for the facility was under review, and although Gloria and her daughter did not know it, there was a strong possibility that the unit was going to be closed down in the near future, and as yet there seemed to be no viable alternatives available.

-o0o-

'So if you and Anne agree, Marlon, what we propose is what I believe is called a "Turn Key" contract,' said the Major.

'Yes, my Gazza will organise the building work to

convert the space, and then do the fit out, working with the plumbers, electricians and plasterers and so on,' added Susie.

'And first of all you agree with Susie where you want everything, like power points, sinks and so forth, before I come in and decorate it up as you want it,' said Magnolia Jon.

'So we pay for it when it is all ready to move in then?'

'Thats right Marlon, other than the ten-percent paid on signing the contract, of course. Then, according to my lawyer,' said the Major, 'what you will be getting is a share of the freehold of the entire place and an individual nine-hundred and ninety-nine year lease on the new shop, which will be yours to do with as you see fit. It has to be done like that because part of the upper floor of the pub goes over what will be a bit of the shop, so it can't be a stand alone freehold. Something to do with not owning the sky above and the ground beneath, I'm told.'

'And will there be any rent or anything to pay on this lease?' asked Marlon, looking concerned.

'You have to make a contribution, which the lawyer describes as 'a peppercorn' to buy the lease when it is set up, to make it legal, but that is all.'

'A peppercorn!'

'That is what the lawyer told me. It basically means nothing, less than a penny if you like. No doubt your own solicitor can explain it better than I can ...' the Major said.

'And then all we have to do is put our fryers and fridges in and so on, stick up a sign and start trading?' Marlon was all smiles now.

'And get the environmental health people to give you your certificate, of course,' added Susie.

'Yes, of course.' Marlon looked from face to face. 'And you really will sell it to us for seventy-five thousand, Major? That's all?'

'If you think that is fair, Marlon ...' said the Major.

'In that case,' said Marlon, releasing his tight grip on Anne's hand under the table and reaching out across the bar to grab a pepper-mill, 'consider it a deal!'

And with that, as everyone laughed, he unscrewed the top of the pepper-mill and rolled out a few pepper corns, selecting one, which he handed with a flourish to Major Harris!

-oOo-

'Yes, and Gazza here is going to organise the fit-out ... he is a carpenter, you know; before I decorate it.' Magnolia Jon was explaining the sequence of events to a couple of people who had called in for breakfast with Eric, the electrician.

'Do you have an electrical layout?' Eric asked now.

'Susie, my wife, is working on it with Marlon and Anne,' said Gazza. 'She should have it done in a day or two.'

Eric, forking another piece of bacon, glanced at his two colleagues, and following their nods of agreement, he asked if it would be possible for them to take on the electrical wiring contract in return for shares in the Community Asset company, when it was formed.

-oOo-

'We are from the Citizens Advice Bureau,' announced the taller of the two women now standing at the bar. 'We have been studying your "Asset of Community Value" application and think we may be able to help each other.'

'Yes, I'm Njoki and this is Sandra, by the way,' said the shorter woman. 'Are you Mike?'

'Thats me,' said Mike, 'and this is Emma, my wife.'

'Nice to meet you,' said Njoki. 'I'll come straight to the point. This area has had no on the spot Citizen's Advice presence for some years, and especially now there is a refugee cohort living here, we would like to put that right.'

'The problem for us is always where we can go to work, if we don't have a permanent office,' said Sandra. 'Your application gave us an idea.'

'Would you consider,' asked Njoki, 'allowing us to hold sessions, clinics if you like, here in this pub sometimes?'

'We think having easier access to some of the resources we can introduce, in addition to advice and support, might be particularly beneficial here, at this time.'

'Can I introduce you to Major Harris,' said Mike. 'He speaks Russian and is giving English lessons to the Ukrainians you mentioned. I'm sure he would like to hear about any resources there might be for that in particular. He has been using children's library books as text books to give his lessons so far, and I'm sure he would like something a bit more structured if he could find it.'

-oOo-

'So, I just thought we had better run through the maths to see where we are at present,' said the Major, after the people from Citizens Advice departed. 'You got a minute for that, Mike?'

'Sure,' said Mike, polishing the bar top.

'Right well, on the debit side, I think it looks like this. I've agreed to pay the brewery one hundred and fifty-five thousand for the pub as you know, and the Knotweed is going to cost about five-thou. Then there is the legal bill I've run up personally, and although there is no legal fee as such for the group, there are those 'disbursements' Arthur mentioned. Costs to stitch all these contracts together and the new company formation, and what-not. Let's call that another five-thou, for the sake of argument.'

'Phew. It soon mounts up, doesn't it,' said Mike.

'Ah, but against that we have to set the sale of what will be the chip shop for seventy-five thousand ... less, according to Gazza, about fifteen to divide it up and fit it out ... much reduced over what it might have been because of all the kind donations of time and service we keep getting ... did you know Susie has been to see the builder's merchant where Gazza had an account before he retired, by the way? They have offered to give her paint, timber and all sorts of other things, and give us sixty days credit on the rest of it to allow us to keep the finances positive.'

'Wow! I didn't know that, no.'

'Yes. I don't know how she managed that, unless she went to see them in that short skirt she wore in here the other night. Susie's own version of the TV show 'Challenge Anneka!" HaHa! Do you remember that Mike ... No? Bit before your time, perhaps.
Oh well ... Now where was I ... ah yes, the debit side. So, as I was saying, we can begin to get a picture of what we have to spend. If you then deduct what we get back from the shop sale from the price I'm paying the brewery, then add back in the aforementioned expenses, I believe we have a target figure as to what we need to raise from the sale of shares as a minimum.

Anything we can get over that helps to pay your wages and the running cost of the place, and I'd like to think that if there is something left over to build a sort of pot for improvements as we go along, we are up and running.'

'Well, I'd need to work all that out with a bit of paper and a pen, Major, but I've also been doing a bit of financial planning,' said Mike.

'Have you now?'

'Yes, If I can nip upstairs and get them, I've done some figures to show best, worst and break-even income projections and a breakdown of the current bar costs. I've also done a little plan to set out how we might improve the takings, and costed it.'

'How have you found the time, Mike?'

'Emma says I must have learned to sleep faster! But the truth is, this is a great opportunity for Emma and me to get back on our feet, and be part of something really exciting, and I want to do all I can to make the most of it.'

-o0o-

CHAPTER 12

Roy Sommers had dutifully called the Managing Director's wife as soon as he got to the office, and said what he thought was the right thing.

Then he rifled through the old man's desk looking for something.

When he found it, he tidied the desk, and was out of his office just before the old boy's secretary came through the door.

Roy tucked the file with all the details of the history and the sale of The Smug under his arm and took it away to his own office.

-oOo-

'Emma! Come here, quick!' called Mike. 'The postman just came and …'

Bustling out of the shower, Emma recognised the heading on the letter Mike held up for her inspection.

'It has come through at last! The insurance money

should be in our bank by Friday!'

'Oh Mike!' said Emma, and as they fell back onto the grubby sofa in an embrace, she noticed that she was not the only one crying.

-oOo-

Barry Beeching decided to have breakfast at The Smug before going into the office.

He had no other reason to go there, except perhaps to tell them about the Managing Director's heart attack, but he wanted to be involved in some way in the busy planning going on. The complicated but exciting business of dealing with the "Asset of Community Value" application processes was fascinating and there was a buzz about the place that was nearly as intoxicating as the beer.

We of The Smug were surprised to see him, and to see Major Harris, who was not a regular breakfast customer.

The Major greeted Barry with a cheery wave.

'Come to sample Mike's excellent breakfast menu, Barry?'

'Hello Major. I thought I would come and give it a try. Bit of news to impart as well.'

Barry explained about the Managing Director but then, casting caution to the wind, he also expressed his dismay that the Area Finance Managers, and in particular Roy Sommers had been put in charge during his absence.

'Well, he can't do any harm, can he?' said the Major.

'Oh, I wouldn't put it past him to try,' said Barry. 'I'll have the full English please, Mike … Hullo! You look very cheerful this morning.'

Mike stood by the table, and with a wide smile explained about the letter from the insurance company.

-oOo-

Arthur, the former Borough Solicitor, had excelled himself.

With the help of the voluntary consultancy firm that he had found and engaged, who had done all this before, he had created a suite of contracts and documents for the group to sign which would form the holding company, register it as a charity, purchase the pub, apply for the Community Asset status, set up the share offer framework and establish Mike and Emma as tenants.

In addition to all that, in co-operation with the Major's solicitor, he had overseen the creation of contracts to transfer ownership from the Major to the group when the time came, and to Marlon and Anne of the new shop. He also done all the necessary background checks into the legal title of the pub, and had created draft contracts for the supply of beer, wines and spirits from the brewery, and finally had set up the methodology for pricing and distributing the shares in the new community business.

As he sat back in the chair at his desk, he decided he was due a holiday after all that, and intended to take one as soon as the deal was put to bed. The fact that he was not collecting a fee for all this work did not trouble him at all, and he looked forward to a time when he could take his wife for a quiet drink in the pub, and possibly enjoy Marlon's fish and chips afterwards. That, for Arthur, was reward enough.

-oOo-

CHAPTER 13

At lunchtime Roy Sommers left the office on a mission to visit the sick.

But not, as you might expect, to see the Managing Director in the hospital.

Roy was on his way to Benedict Place to visit Gloria Glendinning, who held the liquor licence, and despite her current incapacity, was still the tenant in place at The Smug.

-oOo-

'Now as you know, Gloria, you have a non-assignable tenancy,' said Roy, handing her the cup of tea and the little sachet of sugar he had obtained from the machine in the hall.

Gloria was too short of breath to drink the tea, so she put it on the over-bed table, which was a little further away than usual, so she had to stretch. As she did so, she dislodged the oxygen tube in her nose.

'That means, as a tenant, you cannot assign the business to anyone else. If, as has very sadly happened, you fall ill, or if you decide that you do not want to continue running the business before the end of the tenancy agreement is reached, you cannot pass on the business. Instead you will have to reach a settlement with the brewery to organise any early departure.'

'But, I don't want to give up the pub …' said Gloria, fighting to reposition the tube.

'I'm sorry, but the pub is being sold, Gloria. And it might not even open again as a pub. As a pub tenant you know you have no legal or financial interest in the building itself. That remains in the ownership of the brewery and therefore pub tenants do not benefit from, or control, any sale of a property.'

'But what about …' gasped Gloria, still struggling to put the oxygen tube back in place.

'Your personal property? You only buy the fixtures, fittings and stock under the terms of the tenancy agreement. They are yours to dispose of, of course, as is all the furniture and so on in the flat. But, while I will help in any way I can, of course, we do not have long to sort this out. You see the Managing Director has instructed me to arrange to bring your tenancy to an end without delay. Immediately, in fact.'

Gloria gave a choking cough and grabbed at the bed sheets. She was beginning to turn very red.

'Have you made plans, Gloria? Are you going to live with your daughter in Leeds in her flat when you are well enough, perhaps? You get on all right with your daughter, don't you Gloria? Has she got space for you in her place?'

Gloria was starting to gasp and was reaching for the nurse call button, which had slid to the other end of the over-bed table, out of her reach, when Roy delivered the tea and moved the table further down the bed.

'It is just a pity that, as a pub tenant you have no interest in the building itself and cannot control the timescale of any sale. The pub remains in the ownership of the brewery, you see, and if they sell it, pub tenants do not benefit from any sale of a property and have no rights to stay. You will have to move all your furniture out very soon too, Gloria. Very soon. Have you got anywhere to put it?'

Gloria's eyes had started to roll and she was clutching her chest.

'I say, are you all right, Gloria? Should I go and get someone to help?'

Roy got up and closed Gloria's door quietly behind him.

He saw nobody as he walked out into the carpark, through the side door, propped open with a broom; and he got into his car, and drove away.

-oOo-

At lunch time, the following day, Barry Beeching called in to see Mrs Cheshire, the Managing Director's secretary, and enquire after his health.

'Funnily enough, I've just been chatting to his wife, on the telephone,' she said. 'He seems much better and is sitting up and talking apparently.'

'Well, that's good. I'm glad to hear it. I don't like to keep troubling his wife by calling her myself. Perhaps you could mention that next time you speak, and I'll just get reports from you if you don't mind.'

'That is very considerate of you, Barry,' smiled Mrs Cheshire. She had always liked Barry.

'Oh, there was something else I had better pass on to you, I suppose,' she said, consulting her computer screen. 'Apparently one of our tenants, a Mrs Glendinning passed away in hospital during the night. Did you know her?'

'Yes, that is sad, but unfortunately not entirely unexpected. She has been ill for some time. Will you organise flowers for the funeral?'

'Of course. I told Roy about that just now when he popped in. Do you know, I'm sure he smiled. He didn't say anything, except that he would instruct Legal to cancel the tenancy, but he actually seemed quite pleased.'

'Really?'

'Between ourselves, Barry, I don't have much time for Roy. He is always so aggressive, and can be quite rude.'

-oOo-

Little Ivanna was sitting on the stoney beach, throwing pebbles into the sea, when Magnolia Jon and his two dogs encountered her.

Jon recognised her from the English lessons in the pub and noticed that she had obviously been crying and her face was streaked and dirty.

'Hello,' he said. 'Are you OK?'

With an effort, and having wiped her nose on the sleeve of her dress, Ivanna marshalled her thoughts and formed the words she wanted to say, as best she could.

'Is my, ah, mother, she sick. I come look the doctor. Where he is? I not find! Please, no more the dying! What I can do?' and with that she burst into tears.

Luckily Jon had the Major's number, and had remembered to bring his mobile phone with him on this occasion. As he tried to comfort the child, now clinging to his leg, he quickly explained what was going on and passed the phone to Ivanna.

-oOo-

It was fortunate that the Doctor had been on his

rounds, visiting a couple of the other patients, so when Clarice, a carer at Benedict Place, approached him about the sad demise of Gloria Glendinning, he was able to certify the death.

In the kitchen Constable Terry Simmons had popped in for his customary cup of tea as he passed by, on this day each week. Clarice bustled in just as he took the weight off his feet and sat down.

'Something ain't right,' she said. 'Can you come and have a look at this, Terry.'

-oOo-

Deaths in a hospital would not normally require the attention of, and particularly a visit from, the Coroner, but this was different.

Constable Simmons drew his attention to the paper cup of tea and the unopened sachet of sugar.

'Now how did that get there,' he asked. 'She can't get out of bed and it was not time for the staff to visit to give the patients their drink.'

Those in the room looked at the cold and scummy liquid, almost untouched, on the over-bed table.

'Thought I had better mention it,' said the policeman.

'Glad you did Constable, very observant of you.'

'Oh no, not me, it was Clarice, the carer, what bought it to my attention, sir.'

'Perhaps I had better have a word with this Clarice, Constable. You see there is no sign of a struggle, but that oxygen tube, and the tangled sheets …'

'Yes sir. I did ask her if anyone had been into this room, of course, and Clarice, she said after their lunches, that they have early, at half-past eleven, believe it or not; they leave them alone until about half-past three. Thats when they gets their cuppa. That's when Clarice found … found the dead body, sir.'

'What about external visitors?'

'Clarice said there aren't none allowed in the day. Folk can visit from four o'clock like, but she found the body at ten past three.'

-oOo-

'Yes, well it does get stuffy in here. It's that glass roof, see. So sometimes the side door to the carpark gets propped open by the cleaners, like,' said Clarice. 'Especially on hot days like this. But it weren't me what propped it open, sir. I never.'

'Is there CCTV here?'

Constable Terry Simmons was in for a boring evening, scrolling through hours of flickering images on the building's closed circuit tv monitors.

'Should've kept me mouth shut,' he said.

'Never mind, Terry.' said Clarice resting a comradely

hand on his shoulder. 'Would you like another cup of tea?'

-o0o-

Dr Patel spent one half day a week at Benedict Place, on a rota basis with the four other GPs at the practice.

He had been a bit delayed getting back today, what with having to certify that death, so he was just climbing out of his car when a scruffy pink van with ladders on the roof and a very flat front tyre drew up beside him.

A young woman, obviously in some distress, was sitting in the passenger seat.

-o0o-

Sweating profusely, Gazza removed the foot pump nozzle from the wheel.

'Good job you didn't try to drive it home, Jon. I think that tyre would have come right off, if you went much further.'

'D'you think it will be OK to drive home now?' asked Magnolia Jon.

'I should think so. I'll follow you to make sure. And when you get back like, take the ruddy spare wheel out of the shed and put in the back of the van where it is s'posed to be, you numpty!'

'I'd forgotten I'd took it out. I needed extra space for

some wallpaper, see.'

'And how long ago was that?' said Gazza, looking at the moss in the roof gutters and the bird mess all over the van.

'I forget,' said Jon, sheepishly.

-oOo-

'Can you tell her that unfortunately it is almost certainly Covid, please Major. If you give me a moment, I'll hand the phone to her when I have put it in a plastic bag. We will get an ambulance to take her up to the hospital.'

-oOo-

CHAPTER 14

'Although you won't be working directly for the brewery, of course, Mike, you will be responsible.'

'Responsible for what, Roy?'

'For stock-checks and keeping account of orders and deliveries, of course. The Brewery are entering into a supply agreement as part of the deal, and we must decide how to manage the process.'

'I suppose so.'

'Now, by the looks of things, with your food offering and getting all the work done, you are going to be extremely busy, so I was thinking about how I could help.'

'Oh?'

'Yes. You see I have to sign off the returns from all of the pubs after their monthly stock-take, when they arrive in the office. And when the previous temporary manager and his wife were running it we had an arrangement, given that it is on my way home, whereby I would pop in on the evening he did the stock-take, take a look at the figures, and sign them off. If you and I do that in the future, then I could take both copies of the forms back to the brewery office for you, to save you doing the paperwork and the cost of a stamp.'

'I see,'

'That could work very well for you, Mike, and avoid any arguments about shortages or things not balancing, as we could sort it out then and there.'

'We were thinking of taking on a professional stocktaker ...'

'Well, now there is no need for you to do that. We will cut out the middle man, so to speak. I will fill in and sign off the forms and organise paying the stocktaker's fee. That will save him a trip out and be a few more hours and a lot of paperwork saved for you and the community, too.'

-oOo-

When Mike told us what Roy Sommers had said during his visit, we of The Smug were quite concerned.

'That stinks!' said Gazza. 'That little weasel is up to something. I bet he is on the take.'

'Should I tell him to get stuffed, or tell the brewery

what he said?' asked Mike.

'Well, now hang on,' said Magnolia Jon. 'Why not string him along until the deal is done and we need our first stock-take. Then if you think it is anything fishy, if he tinkers with the figures or whatever, you have got him banged to rights.'

'How could you prove it?' asked Biggles.

'Well, Biggles, if two of us attend the stock-take we have a witness, see. If there is any funny business we will catch him,' smiled Magnolia Jon.

'Like detectives, then,' said Biggles. 'Could I be one of the ones to be at th' stock-take? I'd like to be a detective.'

'We'll see, Biggles. We'll see,' chuckled Gazza.

-oOo-

At about eleven that night, Constable Terry Simmonds spotted something on the tapes he was watching.

He had finished the tapes of the hallway, which showed plenty of ghostly images of people moving about, but nothing of any use. The camera was pointed in slightly the wrong direction and was obviously dirty, or perhaps covered in cobwebs, because the images were very indistinct.

The view from the carpark camera was better, although it was hindered by the branches of a tree and foliage which kept blowing over the lens when there was even the slightest wind. But he did find what looked like someone coming out of the fire escape door, which was indeed propped open, at around fifteen minutes past one.

The camera was quite a distance from the door so it was not possible to make out the features of the person, or even if it was male or female. But it was clear that the individual walked over to a car, and when the foliage next blew out of the way, the car had gone, so must have been driven away.

Constable Simmons reported that the car might have been a BMW, and that the last two letters on the right of the numberplate were either 'JP' or 'JB'. It wasn't much to go on, but it was a start.

-oOo-

The Major had established that Ivanna's father was one of the men who worked up at the car-wash, and having received messages relayed through others from the guest house, he had returned from work.

He and Ivanna were sitting now on the bench seat under the window in the pub, anxiously waiting for news.

Ivanna's father sat with her baby brother on his lap, and Ivanna had Augustus the cat on hers.

Ivanna was struggling to stay awake and dozed with her tousled head on her father's arm as Augustus provided his best lullaby purring to calm their frayed nerves.

-oOo-

CHAPTER 15

The news that our former and much loved landlady, Gloria Glendinning, had passed away hit we of The Smug hard.

We knew she was ill, of course, and that the prognosis wasn't great, but it was still sad to hear of her passing, and we decided to do what we could so show our gratitude at the funeral.

'We could have a whip round,' said Magnolia Jon.

So we did.

-o0o-

'I think we are about ready to go,' said Arthur, surveying the mass of paperwork on his desk.

'According to my solicitor, we are now in a position to proceed,' said the Major.

'Our lawyer says it is all systems go!' said Marlon.

-o0o-

'I will be sending through the contract for signature in a minute, Roy. You know the procedure?' asked Sir Jeremy, the brewery's long standing legal advisor. 'Do you think that I ought to just check with the Managing Director before you sign the documents?'

'No need to trouble him, Sir Jeremy,' said Roy. 'I have his full permission to act and get this done, so that we can get on and finalise the figures for our financial year end.'

-oOo-

The two men standing in the reception area announced themselves.

'My name is Detective Constable Bloor, and this is Constable Simmonds,' said the shorter of the two. 'We would like to speak to your Mr Roy Sommers, please.'

While the receptionist waited for her call to be answered, she asked if she could say what their visit was about.

'I'm afraid we are not a liberty to go into details just at the moment, but it is quite a private matter so, if you have a meeting room available that we could use, we would be very grateful.'

-oOo-

The Major had been able to supply some information in answer to the doctor's questions, in his role as translator.

'Her name is Kalyna Klymenko, and she has been working part time as a cleaner at Benedict Place,' the Major said.

'But, to simplify matters, might it be easier just to say that she was unemployed, at present. You see the company with the cleaning contract she worked for don't seem to have been particularly scrupulous about checking the employment status of this lady, and she, as a refugee with very little English, had no idea that it was illegal for her to work until her asylum status was finalised. It would make matters a lot less complicated and stressful for her if you could just put unemployed on your form, Doctor.'

'Or I could simply put "unknown" against 'employment', Major. It doesn't really matter from our point of view, and that way there are not really any untruths. I did not know her employment status, and we might never have had this conversation. And what with the language difficulties …'

'Thank you very much, Doctor Patel,' said the Major.

'Now, if I may, I would like you to explain some precautionary measures we would like her family, and anyone she has been in close contact with, to take, Major.'

-oOo-

'Thank you for taking the time to see us, Mr Sommers,' said Detective Constable Bloor as the boardroom door closed. 'Now then, perhaps I could ask why you found it necessary to telephone Miss Linda Glendinning on the morning after her mother's death, and ask her to confirm when she was going to get some furniture and fittings belonging to the deceased removed from the pub where she was the tenant?'

'I ...' spluttered Roy.

'On the face of it, I must say it does seem a little heartless to be involving Miss Glendinning in that sort of thing so soon after she had been told of her mother's demise. And I am not surprised that she has made a complaint about that, which is why we are here.'

'Well, you see, there is the financial year end ...'

'I'll come straight to the point, Mr Sommers, I must warn you that harassment is quite a serious offence, and the Courts can take a dim view of that sort of thing if it gets to that stage ...'

-oOo-

CHAPTER 16

'What's happening on the Glendinning case?' asked Clarice, as Constable Terry Simmons sat down in the kitchen.

'What Glendinning case? There is no case. You read too many crime novels, Clarice.'

'But what about the tea?'

'The coroner had it checked out, but it was just a cup of tea.'

'No fingerprints on the cup, or the door and whatnot?'

'Only Mrs Glendinning's on the cup, and nothing of use on the door.'

'But how did it get there? Mrs Glendinning couldn't get out of bed ...'

'Perhaps one of the other patients made it for her. You have got a few with dementia in here, haven't you, so it might be one of them.'

'So there is going to be no investigation? No arrests?'

'No Clarice, I'm afraid not.'

'Really?'

'Really.'

Clarice was delving in her handbag and pulled out a slip of card.

'What have you got there, Clarice?'

'It is the door label from Mrs Glendinnings room.' Clarice opened a bin and tossed it in. 'I thought it might be valuable one day as proof I was there, if this case got on the TV news and that.'

-oOo-

'Of course he will have to stay at home for a couple of weeks and rest, but he will be much happier in his own house.'

Mrs Cheshire was delivering her update on the Managing Director's health to Barry Beeching, who had called in as he passed by her office.

'So he will come home this afternoon, then,' Barry asked for confirmation.

'Yes, I'm going over to the house to see him when I hear that he is home.'

'Please do give him my best regards, Mrs Cheshire.'

'Of course, Barry.'

-oOo-

All Roy had to do was print off the contracts, sign them, scan them and send them back to Sir Jeremy, the brewery's lawyer. But his printer wasn't co-operating, and the photocopier in the open plan part of the office, which he could also send documents to, had a monumental jam that had defeated the engineers for two whole days so far.

But he had another solution.

'I have forwarded a contract to you to print off, Mrs Cheshire. I'll come and sign it when you have it ready.'

'Yes, your file has just arrived, Roy.'

'Thank you. Can you ring me when it is printed.'

'Certainly.'

-oOo-

Two minutes later Mrs Cheshire made an internal call.

'Barry, can you spare a minute? There is something I think you ought to see.'

'Certainly, Mrs Cheshire, I'll be right in.'

-oOo-

'No need to bother, Roy. I've just spoken to the Managing Director himself. He sounds quite well, by the way.'

'I'm sorry what did you say, Mrs Cheshire?'

'I said he sounded quite well on the telephone. He is home now and I'm just about to leave the office to go to see him. I'll take this contract with me and he can sign it himself, along with some other papers I have prepared for him.'

'No! I mean, there is no need to do that, Mrs Cheshire. I'll nip over now and collect it to save you the bother ...'

'Oh, it's no bother, Roy, and when I mentioned I had it, the Managing Director said he would like to read through the contract before it is signed anyway, so that is quite lucky and means you won't have to worry about doing it.'

'But ... I wanted to ...'

'Ask after his health yourself, Roy? That's nice. I'll make sure he gets your best wishes and will let you know how I found him when I get back. I had better get over there now though, I'm already later than I said I would be. Bye now.'

-o0o-

'Well you see, Barry, I've lived next door-but-one to Terry Simmons and his family for over twenty-five years,' explained Mrs Cheshire. 'Long before he became a policeman. In fact I used to take him to school sometimes, and gave him and his sister swimming lessons when they were little, so we have always been close.'

'I see,' said Barry.

'Yes, and when this Detective Constable wanted to come to the brewery, and bought him along, obviously he didn't think he could very well come and say hello when he was on duty.'

'What? Were the police coming here, to the brewery? Why was that?'

'Well, that's why I phoned you, Barry. Reception told me that the Police had arrived incase I needed to know, but they said they had come to see Roy Sommers.'

'Roy? What about?'

'Well, that is Roy's business really, but Terry told me they cautioned him. He shouldn't have told me that really, but it had concerned him because obviously Terry knows I work here, so he mentioned it.'

'Cautioned him? Good heavens! What is this all about.'

'Beyond what I've told you, which I will thank you to regard as confidential, I know nothing, but it did give me pause for thought.'

'I'm not surprised.'

'So, I've decided to take what the Managing Director

would call "executive action", to protect the brewery's interests.'

'What do you mean, Mrs Cheshire?'

'You remember that, when he was taken ill, the Managing Director asked Roy and the other Finance Managers to sign anything urgent? Well Roy took it upon himself to assume that meant something as important as the contract for the sale of that old pub you have been dealing with, and now I can't find the file, which I assume he has.'

'So ...'

'So I checked, and really he was only supposed to be signing off invoices and payments and so on. But he has been instructing lawyers and negotiating contract terms and conditions and all sorts. And yesterday he issued a notice cancelling the tenancy on the pub. When I told the Managing Director that, he asked me to find out what he had signed, and by a happy coincidence I had just printed off the contract of sale for signature. So I made an excuse and in a moment I'm going to take the contract round to the house and let the Managing Director see it.'

'Has Roy signed it?'

'Not yet, and he won't get the chance to now, I'll get the Managing Director to sign it himself if he thinks it is OK.'

'I think, following the visit from the Police, that you

are being very sensible, Mrs Cheshire. Would you like me to come with you?'

'No thank you Barry. If you don't mind I'd like you to stay here and keep an eye on Roy. He might not be up to anything he shouldn't be, but ...'

'Good idea. If you have no objection, I will also put in a quick call to Sir Jeremy, the lawyer, just to see what is going on here.'

-oOo-

'Ah, Barry. Are you calling to chase me up? I got held up on the telephone,' said Sir Jeremy. 'I was just about to send Roy a new copy of the contract by Fax for him to sign, and then Fax back; so we can get it exchanged today, which given all the problems he has had with printing the email at his end ...'

'Sir Jeremy, could I ask you to put a hold on that, and call the Managing Director at home before you send it to Roy. He has asked to review the contract personally.'

'Is he well enough to take a call, Barry? Roy said not to disturb ...'

'Yes, and I think he will be glad to hear from you. Mrs Cheshire has just left the office with a copy of the contract that she has managed to print off herself, and is going to see him now.'

-oOo-

CHAPTER 17

'Lately the vaccine programme has become a little erratic in Ukraine,' Dr. Patel was saying. 'But fortunately, as you found out, she had one initial dose and a booster before she came here, so we are beginning to see a recovery from the symptoms, as we would expect with that level of vaccination. She should be able to return to her accommodation tomorrow. But we do need to check the vaccination status of all the other asylum seekers there.'

'Thank you, Dr Patel. The problem is that this family have not had any offers under the 'sponsorship program' yet, so they are stuck in limbo, somewhat.' The Major explained. 'It is not easy to find a home for a family and two young children, and of course they do not want to be split up.'

'Of course not.'

'In fact is the father was a trained chef in his home country and worked in a prison kitchen there, before the invasion, so he should find work easily enough, you would have thought. But the problem is that without a permanent address he cannot get a permit to work, and of course, without work he will be struggling to find anywhere permanent to live. Catch 22, you might say.'

'It is a very difficult situation for these folk. Are they in touch with the Citizens Advice people, I believe they now have experts in these matters available.'

'I don't know, Doctor. I'll ask them.'

-oOo-

Mrs Cheshire sought out Barry on her return to the office.

'The Managing Director and I have had an 'off the record' telephone discussion with my policeman neighbour, Terry. That poor woman!' said Mrs Cheshire. 'Her mother, not even dead a day, and Roy Sommers was on the 'phone hounding her to remove her mother's things from the pub. No wonder she complained to the police.'

'Is that what happened? Is that why the police came to interview him at the brewery?'

'Yes, Barry. The Managing Director said it was disgraceful behaviour and not in the spirit of … of something or other. And by the looks of things Roy is for the high jump.'

'And what happened about the contract for the sale of

the pub?'

'Well, he got very tired when he started reading that, especially after that other business with Roy, so I came away to let him rest, and he said he would call me when he had been through it with Sir Jeremy. Then we will know what he wants us to do.'

'I'm relieved to hear that.'

'Now, if you will excuse me, I have to go to see Helen in HR to give her this note he wrote out for me. I think it might be something to do with Roy.'

-oOo-

'Are you sure about this, Marlon? Blue paint on all the walls?'

'Pale blue, Susie. A nautical theme, we thought,' said Anne, who particularly liked pale blue.

'I'll do it any colour you say, of course,' said Magnolia Jon. 'Just tell me when I can start.'

'Do you have Eric the electrician's number, by any chance, Jon?' said Susie. 'I've finished the electrical layout now and he might want to take a look at it before he confirms his offer to be paid in shares, when the time comes.'

'That time is coming soon, according to the Major,' said Jon. 'As I understand it we might exchange contracts tomorrow. It would have been today, but there was some minor hold up at the lawyers end.'

-oOo-

'Sorry to trouble you, Mike,' said Barry. 'I've just had our Managing Director on the phone raising a query on some points in the legal contract, which he has a copy of to read.'

'No problem, Barry,' said Mike, adjusting his mobile phone between his shoulder and his ear as he poured a pint. 'How can I help?'

'Well look, of course the brewery would be delighted if it was correct, but did you really mean to agree to a three year exclusive supply agreement with the brewery as one of the conditions of sale? We, that is to say the Managing Director and I, seemed to think it was to be twelve months.'

Mike almost lost control of his phone and was in danger of dropping it in the pint he was pouring.

'I don't think that is anything the Major would have agreed to, Barry,' he said. 'He is not here at the moment, but I'll call him and check if you like. I seem to remember it being a one year deal too.'

'And there is something else funny here,' said Barry. 'One of our standard clauses about paying the brewery a royalty from the value of any food sales also appears in the section outlining the terms of the supply agreement. Is that just a mistake?'

'Good heavens! I hope so. That part of the pub's income

will represent most of my wages!'

'And there is also something in the main body of the contract, a covenant, it is called, about no subdivision of the building being permitted without permission being sought, and presumably a payment being made to the brewery ... that is wrong too, isn't it?'

'I'd better call the Major and get back to you, Barry, but in the meantime please don't sign anything.'

-oOo-

Linda Glendinning looked about her.

Her small one bedroom flat was already somewhat over-furnished. Where, she wondered, was she going to put all her mother's things.

The police agreed that the horrid man from the brewery was wrong to be so pushy about removing the stuff, and pretty heartless to go on about it so soon after her mum's death, but there was no getting away from the fact that, at some point, she would have to deal with clearing all her mother's belongings out of the pub.

She and her mother were not close, and had seen each other increasingly infrequently after her father's death, but she had spent her teenage years in that pub, and she knew how big the accommodation on the two upper floors was, and just how much stuff her mother had crammed into it over the years.

It was going to be a daunting task.

-oOo-

We of The Smug, who regularly took breakfast there, liked to gather early. And as Emma manned the coffee machine we were surprised to find the Major amongst those present.

'Good morning Major. Breakfast twice this week?'

'Good morning Emma, just a coffee please, magnificent though your breakfasts are, and popular judging by the number of people here, I'm more of a coffee and newspaper man this early.'

'One coffee coming up. The newspapers are usually on that table, but it looks as if some of our customers are already reading them.'

'That's fine, Emma. Is Mike around? I really called in to discuss something about figures with him.'

'He's in the kitchen, but we swap over in a minute so we share the cooking and bar duties. I'm about ready to tackle some cooking now that I've had my caffeine hit, so … Ah, speak of the devil, here he comes now.'

'Thank you, Emma. Good morning Mike.'

'Good morning, Major,' said Mike wiping his hands on a teacloth. 'Breakfast twice in a week?'

'Well, not exactly. Could I have a word, do you think.'

'Sure. Everyone is eating so I'm not busy now. Shall we sit over there?'

As they took their seats the Major opened his battered little briefcase and withdrew some papers.

'I've been going through the figures and the projections you gave me the other day, Mike,' he said. 'Having spent a considerable part of my life cooped up in an Army Tank and then in a briefing room talking to people about to be driving about in tanks, I can't say I'm very used to figure work, but I have found what you produced quite absorbing.'

'Thank you Major!'

'Well, yes. But I've had to spend a considerable amount of time studying the "before" figures to understand how all the various income and outgoing streams tie together in a pub, and while it has taken me ages to get a handle on it, I think I might be beginning to understand it now, except for one thing.'

'And what is that, Major?'

'The cash movements are complicated, and balancing the tills seems to be something of an ongoing nightmare. The figures prepared for you by Doris Smith as you moved in and those you prepared subsequently do balance, but I found one or two things I couldn't account for. Why, for example, is cat food listed in the cash outgoings?'

'Oh, you noticed that one. When we first moved in Mrs Smith, the brewery's trouble shooter, said we should do a supermarket run and list what we bought in a note which we put into the till, so that we could get started straight away. There are some groceries and some cleaning things in there as well, which are all paid back under the heading 'miscellaneous receipts'. The figures don't exactly match because we found almost fifteen pounds in coins and notes in a jar behind the till. It was probably meant to pay for something but we had no idea what, so we paid it back into the till.'

'Good heavens, it does get complicated, doesn't it.'

'That is one of the many downsides of a cash business, Major.'

'Well, that is fine, but there is one other recurring payment I didn't understand.'

'Go on.'

'Well, it hasn't happened since you took over but, looking at the till returns for the six months beforehand, each month a payment of fifty pounds in cash is made to 'Ace Cleaners'. The odd thing is that there is a standing order in the banking to All-Clean Ltd., for cleaning services each month, so I wondered why there were two bills for cleaning.'

'All-Clean are the company we use, and propose to retain, Major. I've never heard of Ace Cleaners, unless it is the window cleaners ...'

'No. That is Ricky Jones,' said Emma, arriving with the coffee pot to top up the Major's cup. 'He comes every six weeks.'

'You are right. Well, in that case, I'm afraid I don't know what this Ace Cleaners is all about, Major. They don't appear in my projections going forward, perhaps I have missed something.'

'Well, I didn't mean to suggest that, Mike ...'

'No, problem. Look, I've got all the bits of paper Mrs Smith took out of the tills, when we took over upstairs, in a shoe box. I'll just nip up and get it, shall I, then we can see if we can find the receipt in question.'

-oOo-

CHAPTER 19

Roy Sommers realised that the 'Designate' in his job title was unlikely to be removed for a while now, if ever. The complaint and the visit from the police had put paid to that.

There were only two working days left until the books closed for the Year End, and try as he might, he could not think of anything he could do now to get the sale of The Smug over the line in time.

It was possible that the Managing Director would simply sign the contract, of course. But there might be questions to address if he did not immediately recognise that all the measures now built into the wording were entirely for the brewery's benefit. Admittedly they were not part of the original agreement, but so far at least, nobody had picked up the extra clauses in all the rush to get the deal done, as far as he could make out.

Of course the longer period for the supply agreement was a masterstroke, and not just for the brewery.

If that lucrative tweak stayed in the contract, there really ought to be smiling faces at the brewery and perhaps an extra reward for Roy.

He knew inserting the clause from a standard pub management contract about a payment for any food sold was contentious, but he could claim it was just a drafting error and remove it. In some respects he had inserted the standard clause wording as a distraction. If that got picked up it might take attention away from the other little points he had slid in.

His enemy was time, however. He needed that end of year bonus like never before.

Janet, his first wife, had committed to buying two new ponies for the younger girls and had been maxing out her credit cards. He had an idea that since it emerged that Alice, his new wife, was pregnant, Janet had been talking to a lawyer again about the child support payments he had missed. The amount was mounting up, and without that bonus he had no chance of paying it off and getting her off his back.

He wondered, for the hundredth time, if there really was nothing he could do to push the sale of The Smug over the line.

-oOo-

'But it is just a page from a receipt book. The sort of thing you can buy at any stationers. There is no company address or contact details, just a receipt for fifty pounds for some unspecified 'cleaning' and a date. Do you suppose this is all they got each month in the past, Mike.'

'I'm afraid it might be. Any publican worth his salt should have been aware that receipts like that are always open to question, if not asking for trouble, when the auditors come in. It's not a lot of money, Major, but if it did happen every month it does mount up.'

'Yes, it would.'

'Shall I ask Barry Beeching if he knows anything about Ace Cleaning and what service they were providing for cash each month?'

'If you think he might know, that is a good idea. But if we have to face little niggles like this all the time, I for one withdraw my objection to cash-less transactions. At least when cards are used you have an audit trail.'

-oOo-

It took Barry very little time to find a recognisable trail to follow. With the Managing Director's permission, Mrs Cheshire gave him the log-in codes to look at the accounts and till returns for all of the thirty-one managed pubs Roy was responsible for.

Across nineteen of them, a till receipt was logged each month for fifty pounds in favour of 'Ace Cleaning'.

Barry called the Managing Director himself, this time.

'What I've noticed, sir, is that each of the dates

recorded are the same as the stock-taking day.'

'Ask Mrs Cheshire to open the stock-taking records for each of those pubs and see who signed off the paperwork, please Barry, and ask her to report back to me. I think the people at that pub ... Mike and Emma, wasn't it ... might have uncovered something quite interesting. It is a pity we don't have anywhere to offer them employment with the brewery direct. Good people like that are hard to find.'

-oOo-

The space on the first and second floors over The Smug is enormous. The property originally had 'letting rooms' where the manager's flat is now, and the big flat on the second floor housed several 'live in' staff.

Part of the building, on the first floor, is a large open storage area, and two little offices, approached by a narrow staircase to the right hand side of the building as you look at it from the front. The staircase runs up a structural wall at the rear of the building, behind what was to become Marlon and Anne's fish and chip shop.

Susie's plans cleverly separated it from the chip shop with a wall and a new door from the pub's kitchen. There was already another door leading to the narrow strip of land at the rear of the pub, which was currently unused and overgrown. Outside there was a weed-choked path, that led to a gate opening onto the carpark next door, but there was no access from there to the front or sides of the building, which adjoined the bookmakers on one side and was closed off with the wall of the customer toilets on the other.

Mike and Emma were exploring the first floor space with Susie and discussing what could be done with it.

'Well, it goes over what will be the fish and chip shop, as far as I can work out,' Mike said. 'On the other side of that wall is the couple of rooms we use as offices for the business, accessed up the main staircase.'

'That's right, Mike. By the looks of it, it was used as a store when this place was a steakhouse,' said Susie, 'but not for anything much since.'

'It is big enough to be another flat,' said Emma. 'But there is no need for anymore living accommodation. The flat we intend to use has four bedrooms, and the one on the top floor has three or four more, and we have no idea what to do with that yet. I suppose we could use it temporarily to store all the furniture from Gloria Glendinning's time. I can't say it is anything I'd choose.'

'At the moment the top floor flat is just housing spiders and cobwebs,' said Mike. 'We need to ask if anyone has any ideas for what to do with that.'

'Ugh! Spiders,' said Emma.

'You could always rent it out,' said Susie.

'The problem with that is that you have to go through the bar to get to both flats, which is not ideal.'

'Although,' said Susie, removing a tape measure from her back pocket, 'I wonder ...'

Susie measured the wall from the top of the narrow staircase to the point where it joined the wall dividing it from the pub's offices and Mike and Emma's flat.

'With all the effort concentrated on getting the fish and chip shop plans done, nobody has given this area a second thought,' she said. 'Give me a minute.'

-oOo-

CHAPTER 20

'I see,' said the Major, studying Susie's sketches once more. 'So by doing away with that door to the kitchens, and adding a staircase, that would make the top floor flat self contained.'

'Yes. And with no direct access to the rest of the building I see no reason why you could not let it out,' said Susie.

'The income from something like that would certainly help with the viability of The Smug, Susie. But you said there was another idea?'

We of The Smug clustered round as Susie produced another set of sketches.

'Yes. If we can find the money, I think we could convert the store and the area over what will be the chip shop into offices, or something like that.' Susie explained. 'If we used the staircase from the rear, with access off the new landing which serves the the top floor flat on the other sketch, it would also be self contained, with no access to the pub.'

'How would people get into it?' asked Biggles.

'Through the gate from the public car park at the back,' said Susie. 'If we were careful with the treatment of the fenestration design of the entrance there, it could look quite natural.'

'Pardon?' said Biggles.

'She means it will look as if it was meant to be like that,' said Gazza. 'People involved in architecture, and that sort of thing, always speak that way.'

'Sorry,' said Susie, 'I'll try not to do it again.'

-oOo-

Barry Beeching went to visit The Dun Cow, which was run by Steve and Iris Merton. It was their first pub and they were struggling.

'Yes, if it wasn't for Roy coming and helping us out so often I don't know where we would be,' said Iris. 'It's the bookwork that defeats us.'

'Roy has been very generous with his time,' said Steve. 'It is good to know the brewery has been so supportive to us, and fortunate that we are on his way home. He comes every month and helps with the stocktake, which I find quite difficult, as well as popping in from time to time to help us with balancing the till and what-not. As a result we are learning fast and couldn't be happier.'

After that, Barry went to 'The Ship', a large pub and restaurant, run by Gerry and Lauren Crocker. They were also fairly new to the trade, and told the same story of Roy, who they said fortunately lived nearby, helping them out from time to time with the books and particularly the stocktaking.

Johnny French and his partner Graham, at The Cockerel, had a different story to tell.

'Oh yes,' Graham said, 'I mean, I suppose it is nice to know that the brewery are supportive, but do we really need someone here every month nosing about in the office and hanging around watching our every move while we do stocktaking? We feel as if he suspects us of thieving or something.'

The next three managed pubs Barry visited also saw Roy regularly, and always on stocktaking days.

Barry decided he had enough, and returned to the office to make his report.

-oOo-

'I'm very pleased to meet you all,' said Giles Falstaff, the recently elected MP.

We of The Smug were not universally pleased to meet him, and one or two of the more radical members of our little group of thinkers were certainly not among those who voted for him.

'It is very kind of you to call in,' said the Major,

smiling as a photographer captured their handshake for posterity.

'I am fascinated by what you are doing here, and how you have been able to use the 'Localism Act' to bring this place into community ownership,' the MP was saying. 'It is an excellent example of bringing people together and empowering them to become involved in … in … in the community. Yes, Community. Localism. Bringing decisions back to those most affected by them. Government with a light touch in operation …'

It seemed he might burble on like that indefinitely, so Mike intervened by offering him a drink.

'I say! Could I pour a pint? I've seen the PM doing that, and I'd love a go!'

The next ten minutes were spent with the photographer "setting up the shot" and moving us out of the way, before Mike showed him what to do behind the bar.

'Chinless wonder,' Gazza muttered under his breath, just loud enough for we of The Smug, to hear. Now that we were shuffled off to the other end of the bar, our part of the Community had no part in this, it seemed.

-oOo-

'I think it would be an excellent idea,' said Njoki, of the Citizens Advice Bureau. 'The plan, as I understand it would be to use these new offices you can create as a 'multi-use' space, where the local MP can hold his monthly Public Surgeries, and for us to work two or three days a month and store some materials.'

Mike, Susie, Njoki and two representatives from the local Council were standing in the empty storeroom and looking at Susie's sketches.

'If you get the appearance of the entrance right, with appropriate signage, and sort out that bit at the back which is overgrown, I don't think we would have any objections on Planning grounds,' said the taller of the two from the Council.

'We would have to approve proper working drawings from a Building Regulations point of view,' said the shorter one. 'But in principle it looks fine, and a good use of the space.'

'There had also been some talk of using the bigger open area for yoga and pilates classes occasionally,' said Susie. 'And the Major would like to use it, rather than the bar, for his English lessons. How does that sound?'

-oOo-

Roy was beginning to feel quite unwell.

He was coughing and had a headache, and felt his chest tightening up. He decided he might be getting flu, or perhaps just a cold, but in any event, he thought it was best not to spread it around the office, so he took himself home.

The figure work for the Year End was all done and really he was just hanging about waiting for the Managing Director to sign the contract on the pub sale.

Mrs Cheshire had snapped at him when he last called her to ask if there was any news about the contract, so he had to face the fact that the matter was out of his control. He composed a short email for her to explain that he was going to work from home to avoid spreading his germs, but his mobile phone would remain on, and with that he departed.

Barry glanced out of his office window as Roy's black BMW with its pretentious personal numberplate swept out of the carpark.
He could see Roy had on his ridiculous driving gloves through the first floor office window. The staff often laughed at his habit of wearing those behind his back. 'Who does he think he is? Stirling Moss?' was a frequent comment.

As he was supposed to be keeping an eye on him, Barry decided to go and ask Mrs Cheshire if she knew where he was going.

CHAPTER 21

'And then the Managing Director said I was to phone the police,' said Mrs Cheshire.
'They went to his house and collected him, and now he is at the police station being interviewed, as far as I know.'

'Oh dear, this is getting serious,' said Barry. 'Is your friend, your neighbour, the policeman I mean, involved in this?'

'I don't know yet, but when we go home tonight, I'll call in and see him, and try to find out what is happening.'

'Would you mind taking my mobile number with you, Mrs Cheshire? I would be grateful if you could let me know what is going on when you find out. I feel a bit responsible for all this.'

'Now don't you worry yourself, Barry,' said Mrs Cheshire, patting his arm. 'You did the right thing, didn't the Managing Director say so. And this did have to come out eventually.'

'I know you are right,' said Barry. 'But please do keep me in the loop, Mrs Cheshire.'

-oOo-

'I've had a call from the brewery's lawyer, Major. Apparently there is something amiss with the contract and it needs to be re-issued.'

'What's the problem?' asked the Major. His friendship with his lawyer, who was now on the phone, dated back some years and the Major trusted him completely.

'I'm not quite sure, but it seems some clauses were added to it in error and need to be removed. I'm told the new contract should be with us in the morning.'

'Does this affect the contract for the onward sale, that Arthur is working on?'

'Yes, I think so. He is the next person on my list to call.'

'I thought it was all going too smoothly,' said the Major.

'Well, perhaps. I'll ring you in the morning and let you know what they send through.'

-oOo-

Johnny French and his partner Graham, at The Cockerel, had been discussing the visit from Barry.

'You know, sweetheart,' said Johnny, 'I always was a bit suspicious about what that Roy was up to. I never really glanced at them before, but unless I'm looking at the wrong thing, I think this is one of the receipts he put in the till for the money to pay the stocktaker, but it says something about cleaning.'

'Cleaning? You have probably got the wrong bit of paper. There will be another bit of paper in there somewhere about paying the stocktaker that he put in after he had been through and balanced it. I dunno, though. Now you come to mention it …'

'And who are "Ace Cleaners"?'

-oOo-

Emma told us that, this time, two unmarked white vans pulled up outside The Smug very early in the morning and six blokes got out.

The Major had decided to go ahead with getting the Japanese Knotweed removed at his own risk, even though the contracts were not signed and the grant we were expecting from the Council hadn't come through yet. It had to be done, he said, and he would sleep easier in his bed at night if he knew it was properly disposed of.

He had got permission from the brewery to get the work done, and an undertaking that they would repay half the cost if the deal went wrong. That didn't seem very likely at this late stage, so the Major ploughed on.

By the time we of The Smug who liked to take an early breakfast arrived, what was referred to loosely as the front garden of The Smug was halfway dug up and we had to cross some stepping stones to get to the door because most of the tarmac had been torn up.

As we watched while having our breakfast, an enormous skip lorry arrived. It was one of those with large a container on the back and doors, that they use to collect food waste.

The men got suited up in white coveralls and gloves and started carefully putting the knotweed plant itself in the back and then all the tarmac and even the soil underneath in the lorry. They ended up digging quite a deep and wide hole. Then they started spraying it all and one of them said could we use the side door, please, as the chemicals were toxic!

It took Mike ten minutes to find the key of the side door, which was never normally used, and judging by the job he had getting it opened, nobody had bothered with it for a considerable time.

Unsurprisingly, when they started spraying those chemicals about, we of The Smug didn't linger over our breakfasts, and later on, the whole front area was sealed off with wooden screens, about eight feet tall. It made it very dark in the bar, and we couldn't see what they were doing because they stuck plastic sheets over the front of the building and the windows.

The next day another one of those closed waste skip

lorries came and they took away the hoardings and a whole load more of what was previously the front garden. Then they removed the scaffold tower which the sign company had put up years ago, it seemed, and packed up.

But they weren't finished with us yet.

Three of those trucks you see typically filled with gravel arrived and after they had put a thick plastic membrane down, they unloaded tons and tons of hardcore, and then topped it off with more membrane and a deep layer of gravel. Then they used those mechanical 'whacker' things on it for what seemed like ages to set it in place.

It was very noisy and dusty, but when it was done, we all agreed it looked very nice, and tidied up the front of The Smug no end.

It did show up how shabby the paint on the walls was getting, but you can't have everything, and Emma started talking about getting some benches and making an outside sitting area.

Magnolia Jon said they could call it the 'Japanese Garden.'

-oOo-

Darren Spiro from Wideacre Developments had been to The Smug before, of course, but we had not expected to see him again so soon.

'Good morning,' he said. 'I've been hearing great reports about your breakfasts from a couple of our surveyors who have been working down at the sea front, and I thought I must give them a try.'

'You are most welcome, Darren,' said Mike. 'Take a seat and I'll be with you in a moment to take your order.'

Mike thought quickly. This could be a golden opportunity to get more information on the proposal to redevelop and regenerate the area, and the timescales involved. Who should he call?

The Major's phone went straight to answering machine and there was no reply from Magnolia Jon, who probably forgot to pick up his phone again as he went to walk his dogs, but Susie picked up on the first ring.

'I'll have a Full English please, and a latte.'

'Coming right up,' said Mike. Having established whether brown or white toast was required, and when his efforts to get Darren to add black pudding failed, he went into the kitchen.

Susie arrived ten minutes later, just as Emma was delivering the steaming breakfast.

'My, that smells good!' she said as she passed by Darren's table.

'Good morning, Susie … have you met Darren? Susie has drawn up all the plans for what we are going to do to this place ...'

'How do you do,' said Darren, taking in Susie's short, bright yellow, summer dress and long legs.

'I was going to ask how your plans are going. Is it all coming together?'

'Yes, it is very exciting. Would you like to see the plans, I have a copy behind the bar ...'

And so as Susie arranged herself on a chair beside him, we of The Smug were able to watch her go through the plans with him as he ate his breakfast. But none of us expected what happened next.

'So, what are you planning to do with the flat on the top floor?' he asked.

'Not sure yet. What with the alterations for the chip shop, and this new "multi-space area", other than thinking up a way to give it an independent access from the rear, no decisions have been made.'

'Do you think, with the right support, you could get planning permission to extend slightly at the back by the entrance, to provide a lift to the multi-space area and make a separate entrance to the top floor flat?'

Susie looked at Darren in surprise.

'We couldn't afford that. Although the lack of disabled access to the multi-space area was a bit of a pity ...'

'Well look, I may be speaking out of turn, and

whatever I say has to be approved by my bosses, of course, but we are looking for accommodation for workers when the construction phase of our development gets going and somewhere for the site team to meet with the architects and so on. Would you be interested in letting that flat to us for ... let's see, oh, I suppose about three years, at least?'

'Well, I ...' spluttered Susie.

'I'd need to ask my bosses, of course, as I said. It's just an idea ...'

'And is that why you suggested putting in a lift?'

'Well no. You see Wideacre Regeneration, the division of the Group taking this forward, are in the process of negotiating various agreements with the Council to provide some community benefits, on and off the site. I wondered if we offered to fund the lift it might interest them, and count towards the list of off site community benefits we could provide.'

'Blimey! Would you need the lift to go up to the second floor flat?' asked Susie.

'Not really, but I tell you what, if you are interested in this, why don't we start from the premise that the lift is planned to go up there as well. We can always make it just serve the first floor if my company think two storeys is too expensive, or if the planners don't like it.'

'Frankly, I'm stunned.' said Susie. 'From my perspective that would be fabulous. It would deal with the disabled access, the one point where I admit the 'multi-space' idea was a bit weak, apart from anything else. But like you, this is not going to be my decision alone. Can I call the Major?'

'No need,' said Emma arriving at the table with the coffee pot. 'He is just coming in.'

'Good morning all,' said the Major with his newspaper tucked under his arm as he headed for quiet table in the corner.

'Er, Major,' said Susie, 'could you spare a moment?'

-oOo-

We discussed it further when Darren Spiro left, and opinions varied.

'Well, that is not anything I had anticipated,' said the Major. 'At the back of my mind I was wondering if we could come up with a plan to let the flat to some of our Ukrainian friends ... but that is not anything I had worked up in any way. Apart from anything else, as I understand it, generally the Council have an obligation to find them housing, but only once their asylum and so on is sorted out, so they can get jobs.'

'But it is worth exploring, isn't it?' said Susie.

'That idea with the lift is a typical example of how these mega-rich developers buy planning permission,' said Gazza. 'As they might not be able to buy the Planners off with brown envelopes full of cash, although I'm sure that goes on too, all these so called off site community benefits are still just bribes, no matter what whitewash they put on it.'

'Sometimes, Gazza, you need to turn your "conspiracy theory" radar down a bit, mate,' said Magnolia Jon, smiling at his friend. 'I think this is an excellent way to get something out of it for our bit of the community from this regeneration scheme. After all, it seems it is going to go ahead anyway, whatever we might think of it.'

'Perhaps we should vote on it,' said the Major.

So we did.

-oOo-

Prior to getting involved with Gazza, Susie spent her time studying hard for her 'Architectural Technician's' exams at night school, and initially on day release from the company that employed her.

She had been lucky to find the job she had, and her employer was generous with supporting her training. But she worked hard and did her best to deserve the confidence they showed in her.

As a result of the hours of study, the extra work she took on, often staying in the office late into the evening, and the lack of a social life that forced on her, Susie had found no time for relationships.

She was quite short, but was a slim and attractive girl

with large expressive eyes and a cheeky wit. But she never had time to meet anyone, and since college had not really made any real friends. She remained as a singleton into her thirties.

The advent of Gazza, who was at least fifteen years her senior, knocked her for a loop.

She first came across him when he came to repair a broken window frame at the back of the office after a failed break-in attempt. The damage, in the little kitchen area was not very extensive, but Gazza, it emerged, liked to chat. Especially to Susie.

The weather was unseasonably hot when he visited and he was soon stripped down to a filthy vest style shirt and shorts as he flitted in an out of the sunny yard and the office; which was only a little cooler.

'Any chance of a nice cool drink?' he asked, and Susie found him a can of lemonade she was saving for her lunch in the fridge.

'Thanks, darlin,' he said 'Wouldn't rub it up and darn my back could you?'

Giggling, Susie explained that she would not, but she struggled to drag her eyes away from his muscular torso and broad tanned chest as he poured the drink gratefully down his throat.

She should have got back to work after that, but stayed in the kitchen longer than was strictly necessary and made a play of creating a glass of iced water for herself.

'Bet you will be straight in a cold shower when you get home in this bleedin' weather,' he added. 'Lucky husband you must 'ave to come home and find you all cool and chilled, and no doubt supper on the table.'

Susie made some remark and tried to look away, but found a blush building in her cheeks. She had never heard this sort of saucy talk directed at her, and she found it surprisingly exciting.

'No wedding ring, darlin'?' said Gazza returning the empty can. 'Lost it, I suppose. My ex-wife stole mine when she left with most of my other stuff.'

'No, no husband, no ring.' Susie found herself saying, and from there it was but a short step to the exchange of telephone numbers, a trip to the cinema, dinner at a Chinese restaurant, more movies and Gazza asking her in for a coffee.

Gazza kept saying how lucky he was and telling her how much he adored her. Susie soaked it all up and sometimes, quite shyly, told Gazza how she felt about him too.

Now, several years later, and despite the age difference, they were something of a Smug institution. Gazza came in on his own during the week but always bought Susie in for a drink at weekends, especially since he retired and had less calls on his time.

-oOo-

'Coughing and snuffling and all sorts he was, so we had to get the doctor out to him. We couldn't interview him with all that going on, so we popped him in a cell until the doctor came.'

'What happened then, Terry?' asked Clarice.

'Is there any more tea?' replied Constable Simmons.

'Not until you tell me what happened next!' grinned Clarice.

-oOo-

'Yes, little Ivanna is very excited to have her mum home again,' said the Major. 'Kalyna Klymenko is a charming woman, and I've had a chat with her, now that she is no longer contagious. She thinks the only place she could have caught Covid is from working in Benedict Place. She told me she sometimes sat with our own Gloria Glendinning and showed her pictures of Ivanna and her baby brother on her mobile phone.'

'She is not going back to work there, is she?' asked Magnolia Jon.

'I don't know, but I've got an idea on that front. It is true that she was frightened when it was explained to her that it is illegal for her to work there, but you see the family is very short of money, and with nowhere permanent to live, and no 'sponsors' coming forward to offer them accommodation ...'

'You are not thinking of ...'

'Yes, I am, actually. I have a large bungalow with four bedrooms, three of which are unused, I'm in desperate need of some help in the garden, and could really do with a housekeeper ...'

'But Major, that is a big undertaking, and you are living on your own. Supposing they turn out to be crooks?'

'I know that Artem was a cook in a prison in a Mariupol in the Donbas region, now under Russian control, so I thought he might be able to find work ...'

'In The Smug?'

'Well, perhaps. If Mike and Emma decide to take on staff when the deal goes through, and re-open the catering side ...'

'And Kalyna could work here as a cleaner ... That sounds great ... if you are sure you can trust them.'

'I think we do have to offer the hand of friendship to our fellow human beings from time to time, Jon. I can't help thinking of those children, and that we have so much, and they have so little.'

'Well just you be very careful, Major. You don't want to find out too late that Artem was a *crook in* the prison, rather than a *cook* employed there, do you. Presumably there is some sort of vetting process ...'

'I'm not really clear on the procedure and I've got a lot to learn about how it works, but I had decided I was going to talk to Njoki from Citizen's Advice about it, as it happens ...'

-oOo-

'So when the doctor confirmed that it was Covid, he asked him where he thought he caught it.'

'Go on,' said Clarice.

'Well, then I had a bit of an idea, see. He was obviously feeling pretty lousy, and by this stage I guess he was quite feverish and was not thinking straight, so I says can he confirm that he did visit someone at Benedict Place, maybe a Mrs Gloria Glendinning?'

'Cor! What d'he say?'

'How's that tea coming Clarice?'

'Oh all right, here you are, Terry. Now get on. What happened next?'

'That was just before he was carted off to the hospital, and by then he was not talking so clear. But then he says, yes, he thought he did visit someone here, but he couldn't remember why or when. And when I asked again if it was Gloria Glendinning, he thought a bit and then said yes, he thought perhaps he had visited her.'

'Well, thats it then!' said Clarice. 'He got the Covid off

Gloria Glendinning. It's as plain as the nose on your face! He must've caught it when he snuck in to murder her!'

'Whoa there, Clarice! Nobody said nothing about murder ...'

'Am I the only one what can see it,' said Clarice, stamping her foot. 'He might not have even touched her, but when you told me about her daughter claiming he harassed her, it was obvious. He came to terrify her about losing the pub. He frightened her to death, Terry!'

-oOo-

CHAPTER 22

'So, he has asked me to send the revised contract to you, Barry,' said Sir Jeremy. 'I think I have removed all the clauses Roy put into it, and taken it back to what was actually agreed initially, but could you take a read, just to be sure.'

'Certainly,' said Barry. 'How was the Managing Director when you spoke to him?'

'Well, I can't say he was pleased. He wondered out-loud if Roy Sommers had lost his mind, and is going to talk to Mrs Cheshire about getting all the things he was responsible for managing audited in some way, to see what else he has been up to. Given the old boy's condition I didn't like to enquire much further, so we restricted our discussion to the details of the contract I have just sent you.'

'What do you think will happen to Roy, Sir Jeremy?'

'Well, as you probably know he has been arrested, and your HR people have arranged to suspend him for the time being. I think the plan is to deal with it when he gets over the Covid.'

'Is the Managing Director worried about the year end figures?'

'What? Oh no, he said he would take external advice about that. I don't think he is too bothered. The brewery is still making handsome profits anyway, apparently.'

'It was the Financial Year End that was motivating Roy. He was anxious to make sure he got his bonus.'

'Well I think the rest of you might do a bit better when this is all sorted out, if they decide to spread Roy's bonus among all of you. I can't see that he is going to be getting it now.'

'I don't suppose that will happen. But if the bonuses get frozen, I feel for some of my colleagues, who pretty much depend on them each year.'

'How so?'

'Some of the junior managers are on small salaries and a sliding scale of bonus payments and …'

'Well, I'm not going to bother the Managing Director with any of that at the moment, but in a week or so his doctors are talking about letting him come back to work, possibly part time to start with. No doubt he will deal with that then.'

'That is good news, Sir Jeremy. Right, I will work my

way through this contract and get back to you.'

-oOo-

'The annoying thing is that the details of the share offer are now ready, Major.'

'Why is that a problem, Arthur?'

'Well these things are time bound, if you slow it down at one end, it slows down the other. The company I am working with have come up with a quite complicated interlinked timetable for getting it all done, and it is quite a lot of work to do it all again.'

'So costs might go up again?'

'They might.'

-oOo-

'My friend at the Magistrates Court told me the case against him for fraudulently putting his hand in the till to the tune of fifty-quid a month at about a dozen pubs is clear enough, and he will go down for that, Mrs C.,' Terry drew his chair a little closer to her desk. 'But there is something else ...'

'Go on, Terry. Nobody can hear us in here,' said Mrs Cheshire. 'I shan't say a word to a soul, if you want to tell me something confidential.'

'Thank you, Mrs C. It's about Gloria Glendinning.'

'Don't you mean Linda Glendinning, the daughter? She complained of harassment, didn't she?'

'No, I mean Gloria, the mother. There is potentially something very much bigger than these other things that relates to her.'

-oOo-

'Wideacre Regeneration have made a very generous offer to fund an extension and a lift for the multi-purpose room at the pub as part of the Section 106 negotiations, Susie,' the taller of the two planning officers who had visited to look at the scheme said. 'Would that interest your group?'

'Er, I haven't drawn anything up yet, but in principle, yes. We are talking about a three storey lift, going to the top floor flat as well, aren't we?'

-oOo-

When Magnolia Jon, realising that he might be needing his van for all the decorating at The Smug, finally relented and took it to the hand car wash on the main road, he sought out Artem, as the men did their work.

He fished in his pocket and produced a slip of paper on which, at his request, the Major had written a short message in Russian.

Artem read it, nodded and touched the arm of one of the men, who he engaged in conversation.

Then, with a smile and a flourish he wrote his own note on the back of the paper and though a series of complicated hand movements indicated that he had finished.

'For Major,' he said, and that was the end of that.

At The Smug later, the Major looked at the note, and then at Jon.

'Sixty-quid.' he said.

'Pardon?' said Jon.

'If you take the van round to the Seaview Guest House where they all live on Saturday morning, Boyko will service the van and charge you sixty-quid. You just have to supply the oil.'

'Right,' said Jon. 'Does he say how much oil it needs, and what sort?'

-oOo-

CHAPTER 23

'Witness testimony' is evidence that is not supported by physical evidence, but relies solely upon the account and credibility of the witness. That could include an individual who testifies that they saw someone directly commit an offence or saw the suspect in the area at the time of the crime.

'This CCTV footage is not going to be enough to charge him with anything,' Detective Constable Bloor rubbed his eyes as he looked away from the screen.

'Couldn't the boffins enhance it a bit?' asked Constable Terry Simmons. 'I was pretty sure the last two numbers of the number plate were JP or maybe JB, but beyond that ...'

'It might be his car, but nobody saw him arrive or leave as far as we know, or what he was doing at Benedict Place. Without an eye witness, we have nothing, Constable. Just concentrate on getting those bogus receipts from all those pubs so we can submit them as evidence that our boy was on the fiddle. There we do have a case.'

-oOo-

'So that's that, Clarice. No eye-witness, no case.'

'He done it, I know he did.' Clarice stood with her hands on her hips. 'We've just got to find a way to prove he was here.'

'And are you sure nobody else was about? The CCTV of the lobby area outside her door is much too indistinct to be certain about anything, let alone anybody, being around. Can't you get the cobwebs off it so it is some use?'

'I ain't getting up there! Me and ladders don't mix. But I'll have a word with Zofia Kaminski, who runs the cleaning teams, maybe one of them could do it.'

'Were there any cleaners here at the time of the … of the incident?'

'There's always cleaners here. They come and go all day. But they are nothing to do with us, and they are all foreign, like. Polish mostly. We don't have much to do with them. Most of 'em don't speak no English. They keeps to themselves.'

'Could you find out if any of them were on duty at that time, Clarice?'

'Why can't you do it, Terry?'

'I told you, it has been decided there is no case, so

I'm not allowed to get involved. Which reminds me, I must get on, I'm off on a pub crawl … alcohol free, of course! Thanks for the tea, Clarice.'

-oOo-

'Good news, Major,' said Timothy Fisher from the Parish Council. 'We have just heard that we have the Grant and can pass it on to you for the Japanese Knotweed removal as soon as the contracts are all exchanged.'

'Thank you, Timothy. That is a bit of a relief, actually.'

'Oh, didn't you think we would get it?'

'No it wasn't that. You see when things were moving along at such a pace I didn't want the fact that there was Knotweed there to hold anything up, so I instructed the company who did the survey to get on and do the work. So as of this moment, I've paid for it myself.'

'Good heavens! Supposing the deal collapsed, you wouldn't have been able to get your money back …'

'Well, no, I had an agreement with the brewery in place.'

'I thought the contracts for the purchase had not been finalised yet?'

'This was a separate arrangement, an undertaking if you like. They said they would repay half the cost of getting it removed if the deal fell through.'

'Oh I see. Well it would have had to be removed at some point anyway, whoever owned the pub.'

'Precisely,' said the Major. 'I just decided to take the initiative. Good Army training, you see. Leave nothing to chance!'

-oOo-

'Has that old pink van of yours got an MoT?' asked Gazza.

'Well, I ...' said Magnolia Jon.

'Best you check, old son. I think you are going to need it soon to get your paint and that, but also I'll need stuff collecting from the builder's merchants soon.'

'Who says I'm going to collect all your stuff from the merchants for you!'

'I do. We are both working on this for nothing, remember, so the less we spend on getting things delivered, and that, the better.'

'All right, Gazza. I take your point. And you couldn't get much stuff in that tiddly little car you and Susie have.'

'Yeah. Susie's choice that was. When I retired I had a smoking great truck with a big snarly engine, and plenty of space in the back. Now we have this trendy little Fiat thing. Very "architect", but not very "builder".'

'You don't really mind though, do you, Gazza. It's not like you need it for work anymore.'

'I'll be honest with you, mate. When me and Susie got together, if she had wanted me to drive a pink van, I'd of done it. Love you see.'

'Oh do give over, Gazza. It wasn't always pink. It was red. It's the sun that has damaged the paint.'

'Yeah. About twenty years ago.'

Magnolia Jon was about to respond with a cutting remark, when Gazza announced that he was having another beer, and asked if Jon wanted a refill of his coffee.

-oOo-

'I've been thinking about what those two are talking about, Susie, and there is no doubt, it is going to need a lot of redecoration.'

'It is, Emma, but I have been meaning to talk to you about the style we want to adopt. We will have to make proposals to the group, of course, but the Major tells me it will revert to being called "The Coach and Horses" when all this goes though, and the sea-faring theme in the decor currently is not really appropriate for a name like that.'

'Well, you are the artistic one, have you got any ideas?'

'You know, I had this idea that with the traditional fish and chip shop next door, it could stand a very British sort of theme in here. Traditional, but not old fashioned. Patriotic, if you like. A celebration of the British community spirit.'

'That's good. We could put up flags and things to celebrate England's past ...'

'An old butcher's bicycle by the door...'

'A photograph of Winston Churchill with a drink in his hand ...'

'And perhaps a picture of the hop pickers that worked round here ...'

'And some horsey things, of course, to reflect the name 'The Coach and Horses', maybe.'

'But modern things, maybe something from the Riding School for the Disabled up the road ...'

'That's a good idea. And the 'Coach' theme could be one of those pictures of an old charabanc. The sort of thing workers in London used to come here in, for a day at the seaside ... that sort of coach.'

'That all relates to a sense of community, doesn't it.'

'It does. I like it!'

-oOo-

CHAPTER 24

'You see,' said Darren Spiro, 'we need a venue with plenty of parking.'

'And you thought, with the public car park next door ...'

'Yes, that's right Mike.'

'So what will this exhibition comprise?'

'Well lots of pin-boards with the plans and artists impressions on, of course, but we wondered if we could offer some bits and pieces to eat. Sausage rolls, that sort of thing, and complimentary non-alcoholic drinks, perhaps.'

'I'm sure we could do that, yes.'

'There will be a bit of speechifying from our MD, and the local MP, I expect, but nothing too heavy. And brochures to hand out to people telling them about the scheme and how it will regenerate the community. We might also set up a screen and run a video presentation, perhaps.'

'Susie said there would probably have to be a public consultation about your application to redevelop the seafront area because it is such a big scheme. Is this going to be part of that?'

'Yes, that's right. And if we can do it here, it will be right in the heart of the area where it is going to take place.'

'I'll have to ask the group, of course, but on the face of it, I can't see any problem with that. It has just occurred to me ... would you mind if we combined a corner of this with a little exhibition about our own plans for this place ... with lots of people coming that could really help us too.'

-oOo-

'So now that contracts have finally exchanged, I thought we might have a bit of celebratory drink tomorrow night,' said the Major. 'Arthur, the solicitor who has helped us so much, is coming over with his wife, and it would be a good chance for us to say thank you. After all he is not being paid for all the work he has done.'

We of The Smug thought that was an excellent idea, and it was great to hear that the contracts had at last been exchanged. Now all we had to do was set up the share launch, and get people to buy them.

We were going to need to sell a lot more shares than

the one-hundred and thirty-seven signatures we had on our pledge list, so far.

-oOo-

'A Mrs Alice Sommers has just been in,' said the desk Sergeant. 'She delivered this note and said to tell Roy Sommers she would be at her mother's, and her solicitor would be in touch shortly about a divorce. I'd say she wasn't happy.'

'Who can blame her with that little toad for a husband,' said Detective Constable Bloor.

'Drove a nice car, though. One of those drop-head versions of a Range Rover, in burnt orange, it was …'

'Well, our Roy is going to get his fingers burnt again, when she starts wanting a divorce, I expect!'

'Very droll, sir.'

-oOo-

Terry almost bumped into Zophia Kaminski as he was leaving the building, so he thought he might as well ask.

'Whoops! Excuse me. Miss Kaminski, isn't it? My name is Constable Simmons would you mind if ask you a couple of questions about the cleaners here.'

'Is no my business. Bogdan Brzezinski, he boss.'

'Well, yes, that's as maybe. But I understand you manage the shifts here at Benedict Place and organise who works when, and that.'

'Who been talking? I not make work these hours, is Brzezinski. He boss man.'

'No, it is nothing like that, what I wanted to enquire about was ...'

'And this Brzezinski, he do the bladdy wages. Not my problem. I just say them clean here, mop there, is all.'

'Yes, yes, I'm sure that is all fine. I'm simply trying to establish who was here working on a certain day ...'

'Don't talk me about it. Is no my idea, there plenty Polski want the work. Before is all Polski, now bladdy Ukrainians. Brzezinski, he bring them in. Is not my problem. The Polski get the minimum wage proper, but the bladdy Brzezinski, he money man. Who knows what he pay these Ukraine ones, no questions. Ask him, not me. I saying nothing.'

'But ...'

'Is not my business. Brzezinski, Brzezinski, I keep telling. I busy now, you finish? I push off.'

-o0o-

CHAPTER 25

'And so, as of this morning, Major, you are officially the licence holder,' said Arthur. 'As such you are licensed to sell intoxicating liquor in this pub!'

'Hooray!' said Biggles.

'And that being the case, I think I shall have another, and then we must sign off the business plan …'

'On the house, of course!' said the Major.

'No, I insist on paying for this one. You bought the last one. You are never going to make this pub pay if you keep giving the beer away.'

'I don't think half a pint of Best is going to make much difference, Arthur,' laughed the Major.

-oOo-

'So the Managing Director asked me to tell you, Mike, that the brewery now regards this place as a new customer.'

'I see,' said Mike. 'Is that going to put the price of the beer up, Barry?'

'Oh, no. As I understand it, the rates charged will be the same as before. The Sales Manager will be in to see you soon to discuss that and work out delivery schedules and so-on.'

'Right ...'

'No, what I wanted to tell you was that, when we have the opportunity to enter into an agreement to supply a new premises, to encourage the new customer to sign up, we have a series of incentives we can offer. The Managing Director has decided that we should regard this as a new sign-up so I've come to tell you what we can offer.'

'That sounds interesting,' said Emma, arriving from the kitchen.

'I hope so. Have you a moment to discuss it?'

'Yes please,' said Mike.

'Right. Now normally the salesmen offer these things one at a time as tempters, but the Managing Director said that because of the unusual circumstances and to show our support for what you are doing here, I can go through the whole list with you,' said Barry, removing a sheet of paper from his case and clearing his throat.

'So,' he continued, 'The brewery offers interest free loans to replace or refit the bar, and three months of rolling promotional 'guest ales' free of charge. Then there is a complimentary pack of bar towels and beer mats and so on. Also you can have beer pump cleaning materials; Glasses and jugs; and a discount on wines and spirits for the first thirty days of trading. But best of all, and perhaps most relevant here, we offer branded internal and external signage for free, saying The Coach and Horses and showing the brewery's logo.'

'Phew!' said Mike. 'That is extremely generous!'

'Yes. The group are going to love this,' smiled Emma. 'Would you say thank you very much indeed to the Managing Director please, Barry!'

-oOo-

'I spoke to Zofia Kaminski, the manager of the cleaners.' said Clarice.

'Oh yes?' said Constable Terry Simmons, easing off his shoes. 'I hope you got on better than I did.'

'She was initially very suspicious because of the illegals working, and that. She was quite stand-offish, she was.'

'Oh well, you tried, Clarice. Did she say she would get a ladder and give the CCTV camera a clean?'

'We didn't talk about that, Terry. But I said I was not interested in whether the people should have been here working or not, and she got a bit defensive. So I told her, I said, 'I'm not going away or giving up on this Zofia, I'm trying to solve a murder!"'

'Oh Clarice, you didn't say that, did you?'

'I did. But then apart from saying she wasn't working at the time of that bloke's visit, she clammed up, and wouldn't say no more.'

'I can see I'm going to have to lend you one of my police manuals on how to interview potential witnesses.'

'Sorry Terry. Have I messed it up?'

'Don't worry Clarice, no harm done, I'm sure. But perhaps you had better leave talking to this Zofia Kaminski to the police in future, if the need arises.'

'Yes, perhaps. More tea?'

'No perhaps about it. You leave it alone, Clarice.'

'But I tell you, there's been a murder done. Is no one going to take any notice!'

-oOo-

'Kalyna asked me to thank you for taking her to the Doctor's surgery in your van, Jon.'

'Thats nice. I'm glad she is better now. How come Artem and Boyko were able to get out of the Ukraine, Major?' asked Magnolia Jon. 'It said on the news men were not allowed to leave.'

'Some men were permitted to leave on health grounds, apparently. Artem has Type 1 Diabetes and is insulin dependant, so the medical people shipped him out with his family. I don't know about Boyko, though.'

'By the sounds of things Artem was lucky. How did they end up here?'

'To be honest, Jon, these people are still very frightened and traumatised and they don't much like to talk about what happened to them. All I can tell you was that Artem lost most of his family. They had to drive out of Mariupol in his dead brother's car when the invaders started to round people up to ship them off to Russia and goodness knows what fate. They were in a builing that got shelled and he got wounded, his shoulder, I think; so by the sounds of things they made it out in the nick of time. I don't know the full details, but they got to Cyprus eventually where they met British people, and somehow or other ended up here.'

'We don't know how lucky we are, do we Major.'

'Compared to them, we are indeed very fortunate, Jon.'

-oOo-

CHAPTER 26

'Hello, Emma. Are we all right for breakfast?'

'Certainly, Darren. Take a seat.'

'Can I introduce Sam Cohen, the Managing Director of Wideacre Regeneration, and Eddie Libeskind the project architect.'

'How do you do,' said Emma, shaking hands. 'Nice to meet you.'

'Hello, bringing us new customers, Darren?' said the Major unwinding himself from his quiet table in the corner and laying his newspaper aside.

'Emma and Mike's breakfasts are gaining a wide reputation,' smiled Darren, before commencing a new round of introductions. 'While you are here, Major, how do you feel about the idea to hold a public exhibition of the plans of our development here?'

'All for it, Darren. So long as you don't mind us having a corner to display our plans for this place.'

'No problem with that,' said Sam Cohen with a smile. 'I'm keen to hear more about this place, and I asked Eddie here to come along to discuss the idea for the lift at the rear. Not wanting to step on Susie's toes, of course, but Eddie's practice has designed dozens of lift installations and can probably help with technical design and working drawings, if you would like.'

'I'm sure Susie would be delighted to discuss that. Now Darren, didn't you say you wanted to get some pamphlets printed up to give to people at this little exhibition? We thought to do the same thing about our project ... It just so happens that a local printer, young Jake, has been working with us to produce ... Oh hello, Susie. We were just talking about you!'

-oOo-

'I hope you are not wasting my time on a wild goose chase here, Constable. There is plenty to do without following up your girlfriend's ideas about a murder.'

'She is not my girlfriend, sir. Just a friend. Ah, here comes Zofia Kaminski, now.'

'You again? I very busy, you know.'

'I was just saying the same thing to Constable Simmonds, Miss Kaminski. We will be as quick as we can. I'm Detective Constable Bloor, by the way. I understand ...'

'Yes, all right, all right. This Clarice like little mosquito fly round the head, won't shut up. So I telling, just so long it not come out where you got information, clear? I can't afford lose this job'

'Well, that's very ...'

'This Clarice menace say me the date, and I look the records. Is two cleaner working then. Blessings something or other, the black one, very lazy, and one Ukraine, Kalyna, I think. Not know last names. She good worker, but nervous, always keep quiet. And before you ask I don't know where they living or if they legal ... for this must ask Brzezinski, the boss. Not my business. I can go now?'

'Thank you, Miss Kaminski, that is very helpful ...'

'Is Mrs Kaminski. Mrs, understand? Husband in Poland. Goodbye, I go now.'

And with that, she went.

'Well, Constable. Do those names mean anything to you?'

'No ...'

'Thought not. Where can we find this Clarice, then. Might as well have chat with her before we give this up as a bad job.'

'She might make us tea as well. It's through here ...'

-o0o-

Roy Sommers was beginning to feel a little better.

He still felt as if he had been squashed by a particularly heavy road-roller and was somewhat short of breath, but although he thought he might be about to die at one point, now he found he was still functioning, after a fashion.

He sat in the chair next to his bed and re-read the letter from his wife.

Its contents did not particularly surprise him. There had been rows. But the baby news changed all that; although he had been a fool to take out a lease on that great big expensive new car for her to celebrate. He imagined that, now that it was obvious that he was not going to get a bonus, and might not even have a job very shortly, he would soon be facing an even bigger mountain of debts.

He wondered what had happened to the contract on the sale of that pub. Surely, he thought, if the directors would see that the things he put into it were for the benefit of the brewery, things that that half-wit Barry Beeching should have thought of. He had created something good. That might count in his favour, he thought.

No, it was no good deluding himself. They had found out about the nice little arrangement he had with several of the managed houses. That was impossible to deny.

And then that silly woman claiming he was harassing her about her dead mother's furniture. She really didn't get it that he was just trying to help. That made him cross again.

He felt so angry that he ground his teeth and clenched his fists until the knuckles stood out white against the flesh. He was hot, his head throbbed and he wanted to hit something, or somebody. But he must get himself under control. That police doctor was due any minute and would no doubt want to talk about his "mental health".

Roy Summers put his head back and swore at the top of his voice, and until he ran out of expletives and started repeating himself.

-oOo-

'Blessings and Kalyna? Is that what she said?' scowled Clarice. 'Well, I'm sure I don't know either of them. Mind, we carers don't mingle with the cleaners much.'

'You don't remember seeing them here?' asked DC Bloor.

'Not as I remember. There is all sorts coming and going here. And these cleaners, it seems to me, you don't see that same ones twice.'

'Do you give Constable Simmonds here tea regular, when he pops in?'

'Whats that got to do with anything ... Hang on. Now I come to think about it there is two black girls what work here sometimes. Always together they are.

I could point them out to you. I think they might be working on the other ward, if they are on duty.'

'Can we go and have a look, Clarice?' said Constable Simmonds.

'If you like, Terry. Follow me. I'll take you up there.'

'Terry?' said DC Bloor, with a meaningful look at the Constable.

-oOo-

CHAPTER 27

'Well, I have to say this is brilliant, Njoki,' said the Major. 'And you are sure it will be all right if I make a list of books to order from this catalogue? It is quite a treasure trove for someone learning English.'

'There are a couple I thought might particularly interest your group, Major. I have put 'post-it' notes on the top of those pages. You need to tell me how many copies you want of each for your class, and I'll fill out the Grant application form and submit it for you.'

'That's most kind ...'

'No problem, and I don't suppose it will take long, either. They are expecting your application after all.'

-o0o-

Augustus the cat was delighted that English lessons would be given tonight, and arranged himself on the chair at the head of one of the tables when the pupils started filing in.

Ivanna rushed over and lifted him into her arms as soon as she was through the door. He fully expected to remain in her warm embrace until the lesson was over.

-oOo-

'Three new tyres!' mumbled Magnolia Jon. 'Three new tyres, and ruddy windscreen wipers too!'

'Oh come on, it is not that bad, Jon. You can't be surprised, given how long that old van had been sitting there.'

'Well that back brake light bulb is fair enough, I suppose, and perhaps I should have noticed that the windscreen washer bottle was empty, but three new tyres.'

'Well, you have got your MoT now, and you know the van is safe to use ...'

'Yes, but I had no idea how much tyres cost these days ...'

'Given the state of them, that much is obvious, Jon,' chuckled Gazza. 'Come on, let's get inside and go on-line to pay the road tax.'

'Perhaps I should have sold the van when I retired, then all this wouldn't have happened ...'

-oOo-

'Well, I don't mean a proper date or nothing, Clarice ...'

'No, of course not, Terry ...'

'Just a drink to say thank you for your help and that.'

'Just that, Terry. Exactly. Well, that would be nice.'

'I see the pub up from the beach back there has got a new Licensee, Clarice. Maybe they have done it up.'

'What the steakhouse?'

'Yes, that's the one. We could try that ...'

'Just for a drink, not a meal then.'

'Just for a drink as we said, unless, of course ...'

'No, no. Just a drink would be fine, Terry. Not as though it's a date or nothing, is it.'

-oOo-

'Hi Gazza,' called Susie from the kitchen as Gazza closed the front door behind him. 'Come and look at this on my laptop ... The Architect bloke has sent over some ideas for the lift at the back.'

'Right. Jon and I need to use the internet to get his van taxed, Susie, are you going to be long?'

'Yes, but come and see these! Oh, hello Jon ... did your van pass its MoT?'

'Three new tyres,' muttered Jon. 'Three new bloody tyres.'

'Crikey! That one is a round glass lift going up the side

of an office block! You are not thinking of something like that, are you?'

'No silly, of course not. That is just the front page of the brochure … swipe left!'

-oOo-

The English lesson was coming to an end as we of The Smug took up our customary positions for the evening. We had been joined by a couple we had not seen before, who were sitting at a little table by the bar.

'Looks just the same as it always did,' said Terry. 'I had wondered if they might have …'

'That's her, Terry!'

'Who's who? I mean pardon, Clarice'

'That one over there, with that group of people. That's one of the cleaners what work up Benedict Place. I ain't seen her up there for a while, mind, but she definitely works there.'

'Erm …' said Terry.

'Now I come to think, she was a nice one, she was. Used to sit and chat to the patients … if you can call it chatting, given that she didn't speak a word of … Terry!'

'Still here, Clarice.'

'Do you think she might be Ukrainian?'

'What?'

'Shouldn't you go and interview her under caution or something?'

'Under … you really do read too many detective stories …'

'Quick! She is packing up to leave! Grab her Terry!'

                      -oOo-

CHAPTER 28

Detective Constable Bloor shuffled his feet.

He was not fond of having to explain the details of a case to a lawyer, particularly in front of his senior officer. He found Barristers intimidating, even Police consultants.

'You see, sir, we have no evidence until Kalyna Klymenko can be convinced to come forward. When we interviewed her briefly it emerged that it was likely she was in the cleaners store opposite Mrs Glendinning's room, with the door slightly ajar when the suspect arrived and she saw him checking the name cards on the doors before he went into her room, but she did not see him leave. She had no idea anything was wrong, or that he should not have been there, of course. The language barrier meant she just worked where she was directed by the senior cleaner, Mrs Zofia Kaminski, who, by the way, is Polish and was off duty at the time of the event.

'Getting Kalyna to testify is going to be a struggle,

sir, firstly because she is scared that she had done something wrong and would be sent back to Ukraine, or even Russia, and secondly because without a translator she would be at a loss to follow what was going on.

'The Major has kindly agreed to translate for her initially, but as a manslaughter charge is being considered, the police and the Court will insist on an official translator and Kalyna is likely to be terrified of him, thinking he is a policeman trying to catch her for illegal working and might deport her, or something.'

'Thank you, Detective Constable,' said the senior officer, 'What is the legal view?'

'Well, let me see,' said the almost circular little man appointed by the Chief Constable. 'Firstly we have to think whether there is a case to answer. If we are going to lay a charge of assault then we must be aware that assault does not have to involve physical violence. Threatening words or a raised fist is enough for the crime to have been committed provided the victim thinks that they are about to be attacked. The problem with that is that the victim is dead, so we are not privy to what she thinks. If, on the other hand we are going to try for a change of manslaughter, rather than murder, given that there are no signs of a struggle, we need to establish motive, and just trying to cancel Mrs Glendinning's tenancy so the accused could get his bonus might be a bit thin. Although if Mrs Glendinning is on record as saying that she did not want to give up the tenancy and expected to return to work, we might have something.'

'Then there is the threatening behaviour case the daughter wants to bring, of course ...'

'Yes, if she would testify that her mother did not intend to give up the tenancy there would be something tangible ...'

'And, of course we have got him banged to rights for sticking his fingers in the till of all those pubs ...'

'Yes, but while that might demonstrate a somewhat untrustworthy character, it does not help us with the situation with Mrs Glendinning. Do you have anything else at all?'

'Well, there is that bit of CCTV ...'

'Ah, yes. And the Constable who examined it said he could only make out a JP or JB at the end of the number plate. What is the number plate of Mr Sommer's car, Detective?'

'I'll find out, sir,' said DC Bloor, realising he should have checked before the meeting, and blushing slightly.

-oOo-

'The best option,' said the lawyer, might be to bring an action under the Offences against the Person Act 1861, with revisions. That offers us this:-
"A person who without lawful excuse makes to another

a threat, intending that that other would fear it would be carried out, to kill that other or a third person shall be guilty of an offence and liable on conviction on indictment to imprisonment for a term not exceeding ten years."

If we can get a judge to tally that up with the threatening behaviour case from the daughter and the multiple and sustained history of thefts, I should imagine a custodial sentence might be handed down. But then we must consider the possibility of a claim of diminished responsibility … Have you asked for psychiatric reports?'

'Sorry about that,' said DC Bloor, re-entering the room. 'The number plate is 2007 JP. Sommers said he bought it as an investment and it has no personal significance for him.'

'Thank you, Detective Constable. And the make and colour of the car?'

'A late model black BMW, bought on finance, sir.'

'Then I think the CCTV evidence, scant though it may be, very much comes into play. Are we agreed that we should try to make the case that Roy Sommers visited Benedict Place with the intention of threatening and instilling fear into the victim, and such was her weakened condition that she subsequently died?'

'That is how it looks.'

'Good. Well then I think you had better look into getting Mrs Kalyna Klymenko an official translator and finding a way to gently convince her to testify.'

-oOo-

'Hello, Barry. Can't keep away from the breakfasts, eh?'

'You are correct Mike. A full English please, with white toast and a latte.'

'Coming right up.'

'Er, Mike ... how do you go about registering to buy shares in the pub when the offer opens?'

'I'll get you the leaflet, Barry. If you are interested, I must admit the group would much appreciate your input and experience as time goes on. And if you do buy in, you will be most welcome. Thank you very much.'

'Could I have two of those leaflets, do you think, Mike. There is somebody in the office who is also interested, I believe.'

-oOo-

'So,' said Susie, 'I tend to agree with the architect. If the lift only goes up one storey to serve the multi-use space, then there is enough room in Wideacre Regeneration's budget for the scheme to provide two unisex loos for the disabled, on the ground floor of the extension, and a lift with a staircase going round it along with landscaping the bit at the back, where it has accessed from the car park.'

'What, just to serve the multi-space thing, you mean? How are you going to get to the top floor flat?' asked Mike.

'Well, that is the clever bit. The architect came up with a sketch which put a separate front door, on the ground floor, and a private staircase up the side wall of the new lift extension to the first floor. That would open onto a landing and then the stair leading to the top floor within the original structure, but now with no access to the pub.'

Susie pointed at the sketches she had printed off and bought along as she spoke.

We of The Smug nodded in assent, although she had to explain the layout again for certain people who didn't get it the first time. It all made practical sense, and what Susie said was the "axonometric elevational drawing", really just a pencil picture of what the outside would look like, seemed to fit in with the old building quite well.

'And we are quite sure that Wideacre will fund all this?' asked the Major.

'That and refitting the kitchen in the top floor flat, apparently,' smiled Susie.

'Why would they do that?' asked Biggles.

'Because they have sent us a proposal to rent the top flat for their employees to use for three years, with six month break clauses after the first twelve months, at an attractive rent,' said the Major.

'Break clause? What break up the new kitchen?' said Biggles, and everybody laughed.

-oOo-

CHAPTER 29

The next week or so seemed to fly by.

We had a new visitor as the guest of Constable Terry Simmons. He bought along a jolly little Ukrainian lady. She turned out to be called Polina, and she sat with Kalyna and the Klymenko kids during the Major's English lesson. By the time we of The Smug arrived for our early evening libations, they were laughing and chatting like old friends; Polina with the baby on her knee and Ivanna, with Augustus the cat in attendance, of course, chattering away in their native language.

We learned later that Polina was a professional translator, so it was nice for the Ukrainians to have someone to talk to in their own language and then hear her explain what they were saying in English.

Constable Simmons took himself to the bar while they chatted, and nursing a lemonade, picked up one of the pamphlets about the share offer Mike had left about the place, and enquired what it was all about.

-oOo-

Susie had been dancing attendance on some surveyors who measured up the bit of rough land by the gate to the carpark, and a representative from a kitchen company who had come to look at the top floor flat.

The major seemed to be constantly on his mobile phone, and every now and then would smile and tell those who enquired that it was all going to plan.

Darren Spiro and some people from his office delivered some display panels, including one covered in felt for Susie to use, and a big television which they set up one morning, as we who took breakfast, finished our meals. Gazza fussed about putting up the exhibition panels and getting in the way of the people from Wideacre Regeneration, but by mid-morning people were arriving to look at the displays.

That MP arrived at lunchtime with some of the top brass from the development company, and at half-past three, as Emma and Mike set out plates of little nibbles and jugs of orange juice on the bar, the speeches started.

We of The Smug knew this was going to happen, and had been told to lay off the nibbles. But we were surprised when someone from the local commercial radio station arrived and interviewed the Major about the share offer with a microphone and something that looked like an enormous tape recorder.

Barry Beeching bought in an older lady one evening and took her on a bit of a tour with Mike, and the next day, at lunchtime he came in again with a frail looking elderly couple and repeated the process.

Several strangers came in for drinks, and at breakfast time it went mad, with people actually queueing up for tables, although Mike did reserve a few for we of The Smug, and Emma made sure that we did not have to wait too long to be served.
The Major beamed at everybody and seemed to be constantly shaking hands.

Emma went to the garden centre and bought some plants and bushes in pots, with her own money. She put them in the newly resurfaced front 'garden' and discussed where to put picnic benches with Susie, when the pub was officially 'ours'.

Then Linda Glendinning arrived with Constable Simmonds and we all made appropriate noises about her mother and said how sorry we were, before Emma took them upstairs for a look at the flats.

All in all, it was a fascinating time at The Smug.

-oOo-

CHAPTER 30

There had been a hearing where all he had to do was confirm his name and address, but Roy Sommers actual case was due to be heard at eleven o-clock on the fateful day.

On that morning, various witnesses filed in and sat on the benches outside the courtrooms.

Barry recognised several of the publicans he had visited recently, and then, when he arrived a little later, he stood and shook the hand of Sir Jeremy, the brewery's solicitor.

Earlier, when we of The Smug realised that Mike and the Major were going along to the hearing, some of us decided to tag along too, and four rode in Gazza's funny little car with three squashed into Magnolia Jon's pink van.

-o0o-

Roy Sommers chose to plead guilty, which probably saved him from a very much longer stay in prison, but he was not to find out how long he was to be detained until the lawyers had picked over his life and the experts had reported on their assessments of his sanity.

In Court, we of The Smug listened as the lawyers held their cross-examinations, calling various witnesses, and looking in depth into the situation. And then we sat enthralled as they discussed the expert advice they had taken on his state of mind.

There was some discussion about whether he was going to try to enter a plea of diminished responsibility due to stress, and push to get a reduction in his sentence due to his mental health.

It emerged that Roy's all encompassing driving ambition was also threatening to be the downfall of his private life, and now that was coming apart too.

As part of the background checks, Janet, his first wife, had been interviewed and a statement was read out on her behalf explaining that she had divorced him after repeated incidents where his anger and frustration at his lack of progress at work had boiled over into aggression, and she was fed up with dodging the blows as he became increasingly unpredictable. It emerged that their rows had led to the police being called by a neighbour at one point.

Then his timid second wife was called to give evidence. She stated that she met him eighteen months after his divorce, and they established that she was working behind the bar in one of the brewery's pubs. It was explained that she was considerably younger than Roy, and as a vicar's daughter, was bought up and educated in a private girl's school. She explained to The Court in a quiet voice that, when she met him, she had little experience of the world.

She was at college and on holiday when she took the job in the pub to earn a few pounds, and Roy latched onto her almost on the day she started work. She was shy and retiring, and with only a brief relationship with a nineteen-year-old boy when she was sixteen, and a long distance relationship with a pen-pal who she met on a trip with the church choir, up to that point she had very little experience of men.

The lawyer explained to The Court on her behalf that she was not initially aware that Roy's approach was unusual, and just assumed that his behaviour in the bedroom was what men did. As he never actually hit her, she convinced herself that this was love and that perhaps he would calm down and change, if she let him vent his anger verbally, when he was with her.

The defence lawyer then said that, for his part, Roy suffered periods of great remorse after he had been rough with her, and constantly bought her presents, new clothes and expensive holidays, to accompany his apologies and promises to change. But the Prosecution asked if it was not true that when Roy became angry and the red mist descended, she soon became his verbal punch bag again, at least until it was discovered that she was pregnant.

Reports were read out which showed the pregnancy did change things for the better for a while, and Roy treated her with much more respect. But as the financial year end loomed at the brewery, and Roy's fears that his annual bonus would not cover his rapidly ballooning expenditure increased, so did the rows. Under questioning again, his wife explained that they held shouting matches that lasted two or three days, and although Roy managed to restrain himself physically, it was clear that their marriage was on the rocks since Alice decided to fight back, at least verbally, for the sake of her baby. Another incident of a neighbour calling the police about the shouting was mentioned.

Two experts then took the stand in quick succession, and stated that they doubted that Roy's history and state of mind was sufficient grounds to allow any plea relating to his mental state, and recommended that the trial proceed as normal.

For Roy the future looked bleak.

The trial was an ordeal for others too.

When her turn came to take the witness stand, Kalyna Klymenko was shaking with fear, but she got through it with encouragement from Polina, the official translator, and began to relax when the Judge explained that this case had nothing to do with her working illegally at Benedict Place, and congratulated her for fighting down her nerves and going through with the ordeal.

-oOo-

Things were much happier at The Smug and the share offer was a huge success.

Arthur, the solicitor, and the Major were almost dancing in the bar when the returns were in. But, of course, that could have been all the scotch and soda they got through.

We of The Smug watched in awe as the voluntary organisation Arthur had bought in managed it all, and as the money mounted up we began to realise that the future of The Smug, or The Coach and Horses as it was about to become, was assured.

Marlon and Anne took up residence at one end of the bar, pretty much in what was to become their fish and chip shop, and marvelled at it all.

Susie celebrated when the planning application for the sub-division to create their shop and the new extension for the lift was approved, and the Major bought Prosecco to celebrate our good fortune, which did not impress we of The Smug, who habitually drink beer.

All in all, the future looked rosy.

-oOo-

Artem's "try out" in the kitchen with Mike worked well. He produced an elegantly presented fish dish and, without being asked, also prepared a delicious Yabluchnyk, a traditional Ukrainian Apple Cake, which we of The Smug throughly enjoyed, when it was portioned up and handed round.

The time Polina had spent with the family had enabled Mike, Emma and the Major to understand that before he worked as a cook at a Ukrainian prison, he was a junior chef at a catering college, where he learned his craft.

-oOo-

Now that Njoki, and the other Citizen's Advice staff, had established and stabilised the family's status as asylum seekers, it would be only a matter of time before they were offered the 'right to remain' in England. As soon as that happened Artem would be offered a job in the kitchens and Mike and Emma would start to expand. First with modest lunches and then, if there was enough interest, evening meals.

The Major had offered the family a home and very soon they would be able to move out of the Seaview Guest House and into his spacious bungalow.

-oOo-

Linda Glendinning became a regular visitor. She agreed that her mother's furniture, which was tired and had little value, could be moved into the top floor flat for the use of the construction workers, and the rest of her stuff was taken to auction, or given to charity.

-oOo-

Magnolia Jon checked his brushes, went to collect the paint that Susie had talked the builders merchant into donating, and collected some timber and other materials for Gazza, in the pink van.

-oOo-

With a whisper rather than a roar, it was done. We owned the pub!

Now the real work started and the planning for the party could begin.

-oOo-

As Emma and Mike paused their personal furniture shopping for their flat, and went to buy some picnic benches for what we laughingly called 'The Japanese Garden', Gazza put up plastic floor to ceiling sheeting on battens, to keep the dust down, and began building a dividing wall to separate up Marlon and Anne's chip shop.

Eric the electrician arrived with his plumber friends, and checking Susie's plans, prepared to start work.

Darren Spiro told us that Wildacre Regeneration had received planning consent for its sea-front redevelopment scheme, and the first of the workmen joined the queue for breakfast each morning.

-oOo-

CHAPTER 31

The plans for the 'official opening' were coming together nicely.

Although not all of we of The Smug approved, the Major had asked that bumbling twerp of an MP, Giles Falstaff, to do the honours and declare the place officially open, at the 'do'. As a result, we were all dispatched once again to deliver more leaflets around the town inviting folk to the event.

This time the cost of printing was covered by the special fund that had been set up for 'expenses' using some of the share sale money. That fund was also going to pay for drinks and nibbles at the opening, which Mike warned we of The Smug to keep our fingers off until the MP had given his speech and cut the red ribbon he proposed should be draped over the door.

Preparations for the event took a little while, but the agency the group had used to help us with the share offer, and before that with the 'asset of community value' arrangements, wanted to be involved and put up display boards and an 'information station' in the same place Wideacre Regeneration had set up their mini exhibition.

Darren Spiro was in almost every day introducing various people from Wideacre's development to Mike and Emma's breakfasts, as well as meeting with Susie to discuss the construction of the lift extension and the alterations which were now well underway.

Gazza was banging and crashing behind the plastic dust barrier, which stretched from the back of the bar to the front wall, to create Marlon and Anne's new fish and chip shop. He had opened up the original street door so that Eric, the electrician, and his mates could come and go and bring in building materials without going through the bar. The dividing wall was up, on the other side of the plastic sheets, which would shortly be removed so that Magnolia Jon could start decorating it.

Susie had been busy creating what she called 'swatches' with Magnolia Jon and Emma in particular, to agree the new 'theme' of the revitalised and renamed Coach and Horses where decoration was also due to start.

Barry Beeching bought along various people from the brewery to discuss no doubt complicated things with Mike, and introduced us all to a sign maker who was going to put up new signs and remove the half finished "The Smug ..." lettering. He planned to replace it with a much nicer new sign on the front of the building.

-oOo-

At last the time was approaching for the official opening event.

The odour of fresh paint was still in the air when the new wall was now revealed in the bar, but the smell was much worse in Marlon and Anne's new shop, where Gazza and Magnolia Jon were feverishly working until late into the night to get the building ready for the impending delivery of the fryers, fridges and all the paraphernalia the new chip shop would require.

The plan was to offer visitors to the opening event the chance to sample fish and chips next door, and Marlon, on his visits to the bar, was becoming very stressed about getting his premises ready in time. He began to relax, however, after the man from the Council came and gave him his certificate to be able to trade, and Anne, who visited every day, was able to reassure him that everything was going well.

Susie would have liked to hold the opening event when the pub was completely done up and redecorated, but that was not practical, and she had to accept that the event would only showcase the intention for the rebranding and so-on. So she prepared a little exhibition of her own with thick cardboard posters showing rather clever painted views of what the interior would look like. To add to that, the brewery provided branded materials such as bar towels, beer mats and even the swinging sign that would eventually go up outside by the road to make it all more realistic.

'I'm jus' hoping this new blinkin' sign writer don't go bust before the new signs are all done, this time!' said Biggles.

-oOo-

Mike had new tills delivered that, to we of The Smug at least, looked like something out of science fiction rather than just receptacles for money. They came with colourful blinking screens and little tags on bits of elastic that the bar staff had wear on belts, and touch the tills with, to make the drawer open and give us our change.

The old 'one-armed bandit', which had stood forlornly in a corner by the gent's loos and hadn't worked as long as anyone could remember, was removed and replaced by a pair of sort of a computer game things, that Emma told the delivery man to alter so they didn't keep beeping and playing little tunes while we were trying to have a quiet drink.

The Major explained to us that these gadgets were what he called a 'necessary evil' to help the viability of the bar, and could make us plenty of money.

We all looked on askance as Biggles approached the flashing and glowing screens and began to deftly extract money in the form of winnings almost immediately, and declared the machines a great success.

However, nobody else who had a go had any success at all!

-oOo-

The demand for Mike and Emma's breakfasts, meanwhile, had gone mad.

Each morning there were queues of construction workers and tradesmen of all types on the doorstep as soon as they opened for business, and with Mike and Emma both having to cook to keep up with demand, we of The Smug were pressed into service to take orders and deliver plates of food.

Even the Major found himself, little pad in hand, taking orders, and whilst Biggles was confined to delivering plates of food following a couple of unfortunate mix ups, everyone pitched in to help.

Susie helped in the kitchen sometimes and even Eric, the electrician, took orders from customers when it became really busy.

The new tills rattled with coins, which pleased Mike, and the Major welcomed the new customers and chatted cheerfully to them all, which made them feel welcome and ensured they were likely to come back. As this element of the business started to become very successful everyone was pleased.

-oOo-

Marlon and Anne were delighted with their new shop and Susie even found time to paint some stylised fish on the walls, and make internal signage and a menu for the window of 'Marlon's Fish & Chips' featuring the same little fish.

Anne went shopping with Emma and bought some elegant metal garden chairs and matching tables to adorn the little area in front of the shop, so people had somewhere to sit and wait for their orders, if the weather allowed.

She also went somewhat overboard by purchasing rather too many pot plants, for use inside and outside the shop, and had to take several home when no space could be found for them.

The Major declared that the shop looked 'Splendid', and thanked Marlon for transferring the money to complete the transaction promptly.

Magnolia Jon, having initially expressed concern about all that pale blue, announced that he was proud of the result, and he and Gazza were more than happy to be offered the first 'sample' fish and chip dinners from the newly installed fryers.

-oOo-

The day of the Grand Opening had finally arrived, and although the morning was overcast, the frenetic activity inside the building raised the temperature by several degrees.

We of The Smug were engaged variously to help set out plates of nibbles all along the bar; help Susie to hang her cardboard panels on the new wall, and balance the new heavy swinging sign destined to be positioned on the post by the road, in her display; and then generally clean, tidy, and arrange tables and chairs.

The Major welcomed the dignitaries, including the local Mayor, several people from the Council, and that MP again who made a fuss about having his picture taken in various poses around the bar, in Marlon and Anne's shop, and outside where the ribbon had been set up across the doorway.

Then quite a rush of interested people started flooding in, and Mike had a job keeping them off the nibbles, which were covered up with tablecloths but still attracted attention as he poured the drinks.

Emma was directing operations in the kitchen and Magnolia Jon, Biggles and Gazza were employed ferrying plates of hot tasty bits and pieces and handing them round to the visitors, with paper serviettes, as the moment came for the cutting of the ribbon.

The Major first tried polite coughing to get attention, but ended up banging a spoon on an empty glass until the noise died down and he said a few words of welcome.

-oOo-

When the MP finally stopped talking and cut the ribbon, the Major offered him and the other important people first go at the nibbles on the bar and gave them a free drink.

We of The Smug were surprised at how the people from the Council in particular loaded up their plates and then queued up for second helpings.

Gazza said we should elbow them aside and get in there, so we did.

-oOo-

The MP cleared off after a while with his entourage, and Mike put some music on.

Some of the people from the Council went too, but several stayed on and kept revisiting the food and helping themselves. Magnolia Jon said maybe they starve Council workers these days, but Gazza said it was their natural greed that kept their noses in the trough.

Eventually, when the food ran out, they all went too. That just left we of The Smug, some local people who had bought shares, the lawyer, and the people from the agency who helped us buy the pub, along with someone from the local paper.

At a signal from the Major, Mike started filling our

glasses and explained that these drinks were on the house.

-oOo-

'I dunno what time I got home,' said Biggles as he took his customary place for breakfast. 'But I ain't half got a head on me this morning.'

'Me too,' said Susie. Eric the electrician nodded in agreement, and immediately regretted it, going back to sitting with his head in his hands as before.

The Major, however, was full of the joys of spring.

'Perhaps he is still pissed,' said Magnolia Jon, who only ever drank coffee.

'Probably. Wish I was,' said Gazza.

'Come along now gentlemen and ladies,' said the Major. 'Look sharp, I'm sure Mike and Emma could do with some help with the breakfasts …'

The collective groan from we of The Smug was deafening.

-oOo-

EPILOGUE

Roy Sommers was found guilty of harassing Linda Glendinning. Then he was found guilty of the thefts from the various pubs.

The prosecution proved that an "intentional and unlawful act" had been committed with regard to Gloria Glendinning and that "it was an act which all sober and reasonable people would inevitably realise must subject the victim to risk of harm".

The judge agreed that Roy's conduct took the form of "an unlawful act involving a danger of some harm that resulted in death", and thus Roy was convicted of manslaughter.

He was sent to prison for ten years.

-o0o-

We of The Smug were delighted when Susie told us the bar of the rebranded Coach and Horses was to be divided into two sections, one for dining, to be branded 'The Major's Table', and one for drinking, which was to be called 'The Smug'! Emma promised to have a sign made up saying 'The Smug' to put up over the bar.

-oOo-

We helped Barry Beeching celebrate when he was promoted to the Board of the brewery. No period with Director 'Designate' in *his* job title. Straight in, and appointed as Property Director with a seat next to the Managing Director at the boardroom table.

Clarice and Constable Simmons came in for a drink on that day too, and have been in several times since.

Both Mrs Cheshire and the Managing Director bought shares in 'The Coach and Horses' and we hope to be able to invite them to the opening night of the restaurant to be called 'The Major's Table', when Mike and Emma find time to set it all up.

So now, if you are down our way, we of The Smug invite you to visit 'The Coach and Horses', our very own community pub, and in the near future come to our restaurant. We think you will like it, and we look forward to seeing you!

-oOo-

===
======

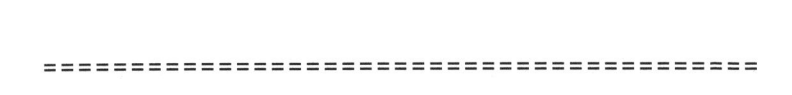

Fancy rescuing your local pub?

[Information reproduced with thanks to Plunkett UK, the Foundation which was used as a reference point in this story.]

Community pubs are owned and run democratically by members of their community.
Community pubs have an open and voluntary membership, giving members part ownership of the community business. Community pubs actively encourage individuals from their community to become members by purchasing membership shares, the cost of which are set at an accessible level that the majority of the community will be able to afford. Community pubs are set up on a 'one member one vote' basis rather than 'one share one vote'. This means that all members have an equal say in how they want their local pub to be run, regardless of the number of shares they purchase.
Community pubs are being established in both rural and urban communities, and the motivation for doing so will be much the same. For some, the main motivation will be to safeguard the only remaining pub left in a local community, or to save a valued asset from redevelopment. For others, it will be to establish a high quality service that meets local needs. The major benefit in all cases will be the creation of a community hub in which all members of a community can come together, interact and socialise.
Like any business, a community pub aims to be profitable. However, the primary trading purpose of a community pub is to provide benefits for its local community. Many community pubs, for example, host a wide range of additional services that benefit the community which may include;
Grocery shop
Post Office services
Allotments and growing spaces
Library and book exchanges
Child care facilities
IT provision

Formal meeting rooms
Social club
Cafes and other informal social space.
There are a number of management options for community pubs. In the majority of cases, the community will purchase the freehold of the pub in order to retain community control of the asset. Once owned, the community have the option of leasing the operations of the pub business to a tenant or running it themselves with either paid staff or volunteers. A lesser number of communities for whom purchasing the freehold is not an option, will purchase the leasehold of the pub, to at least ensure the pub is run for community benefit in the short term, and possibly with a view to purchasing the property in the future.

There are a range of legal structures appropriate for community pubs, but the majority are registered as either Co-operative or Community Benefit Societies, which can reinvest profits in the business, donate their surplus back to the community, or distribute interest to their members.

Plunkett UK has worked with the majority of community pubs currently trading and in the process of setting up. It is the only national organisation supporting the development of community pubs in the UK.

Alongside their advice line, Plunkett can offer free support to any community within the UK via a dedicated staff team, network of regional advisers, mentors and specialist consultants. Plunkett also hosts an online community pub Facebook Group and a website with advice sheets and a range of resources. In addition to this, Plunkett holds networking and training events for community pubs.

By contacting the advice line at the outset, Plunkett will be able to advise you of the current support available, signpost you to the most relevant information and resources, and help to clarify the next steps you need to take to get your project off the ground.

For more information visit: www.plunkett.co.uk

====================

**Fancy trying Artem's Yabluchnyk
(Ukrainian Apple Cake)?
Here is a recipe for this delicious moist cake:-**

1 ½ cups all-purpose flour
¼ cup white sugar
¼ teaspoon salt
2 teaspoons baking powder
½ cup butter
1 egg, beaten
⅓ cup cream
4 large apple - peeled, cored and thinly sliced
2 tablespoons cold butter
½ cup brown sugar
2 tablespoons flour
2 teaspoons ground cinnamon

Preheat oven to 375.
Lightly butter an 8 inch square baking dish.
Sift together 1 1/2 cups flour, sugar,
salt, and baking powder.
Cut in 1/2 cup of butter until the mixture is crumbly.
Stir together the egg with the cream and gently
mix into the flour until a soft dough has formed.
Press into prepared baking dish. Layer the apples
into the dish overlapping, in neat rows.
Prepare streusel by mixing the brown
sugar, 2 tablespoons flour, and cinnamon
together in a small bowl.
Cut in 2 tablespoons butter until

the mixture is crumbly.
Sprinkle over apples.

Bake in preheated oven until apples have softened, and topping has browned, about 25 minutes.

Great on its own served warm, but maybe try it with vanilla ice-cream, if you like.

(Source: https://redcipes.com/recipe/ukrainian-apple-cake-yabluchnyk-olga-drozd/)

=====================

UKRAINE HISTORIC/POLITICAL BACKGROUND USED TO CREATE THIS STORY (Sources: Various newspapers, TV News, BBC resources, Wikipedia and elsewhere).

An ongoing refugee crisis began in Europe in late February 2022 after Russia's invasion of Ukraine. Over 6 million refugees fleeing Ukraine were recorded across Europe, while an estimated 8 million others had been displaced within the country by late May 2022. Approximately one-quarter of the country's total population had left their homes in Ukraine by the end of March.
90% of Ukrainian refugees were women and children, while most Ukrainian men between the ages of 18 and 60 were banned from leaving the country. By 24 March, more than half of all children in Ukraine had left their homes, of whom a quarter had left the country.
The invasion caused Europe's largest refugee crisis since World War II.

On 12 March 2022, British Member of Parliament, Michael Gove announced the "Homes for Ukraine" scheme whereby Britons who offered their home to Ukrainian refugees would receive £350 a month.
On 28 March the Home Office announced it had issued 21,600 visas under the "Ukraine Family Scheme", under which refugees could join close family members already resident in the UK.
The UK government was criticised, however, for the slow and bureaucratic procedures in the "Homes for Ukraine" scheme previously announced by Michael Gove.
The heads of the Refugee Council, the British Red Cross, Save the Children and Oxfam made a statement warning that the system was "causing great

distress to already traumatised Ukrainians".
2,500 applications for visas under this scheme had been approved by 30 March.

In April 2022, The Times revealed that female refugees may be at risk of being exploited by UK men offering to be their hosts, with some proposing sexual relationships or even marriage. On 13 April, UNHCR asked the United Kingdom to stop pairing single British men with lone Ukrainian women refugees under the "Homes for Ukraine" scheme because the women were at risk of sexual exploitation.

By 8 April, a total of 12,000 Ukrainian refugees had entered Britain. 1,200 of them under the "Homes for Ukraine" scheme for those who were sponsored by UK hosts and 10,800 under the Ukrainian family scheme for those with prior family connections to the UK. The British government had received 79,800 applications for visas from Ukrainians and had issued 40,900 up to 7 April, but only 21,600 refugees had actually entered the UK by 22 April and 27,100 under both schemes. By 29 May this figure had reached 65,700.

As of September 2022, Human Rights Watch documented that Ukrainian civilians were being forcibly transferred to Russia. The UN Human Rights Office stated "There have been credible allegations of forced transfers of unaccompanied children to Russian occupied territory, or to the Russian Federation itself." More recently, over 4.5 million Ukrainians have returned to Ukraine since the beginning of the invasion.

-oOo-

12 December 2022: By Lucy Manning and Larissa Kennelly
BBC News
"About 51,000 people who came to the UK under the Homes For Ukraine scheme have now reached the end of their six-month sponsorship period, the BBC has found.
UK sponsors agreed to house Ukrainians for a minimum of six months - and BBC analysis suggests almost half of those who arrived under the scheme have now reached the end of their sponsorship.
Councils say some are already homeless after leaving their sponsors' homes. The government says it is working to ensure they all have somewhere to live. The scheme, which was launched in March, allowed Ukrainians who were fleeing the war with Russia to come to the UK - if a sponsor agreed to provide accommodation for at least six months.
As that period ends for many Ukrainians, some councils have increased the £350-a-month payment sponsors have received to encourage more households to keep housing Ukrainians.
But it is not a national policy. And many hosts and their guests aren't sure what the plan is at the end of six months.
It comes as the latest figures - up until 18 November - show more than 2,000

Ukrainian families with children, as well as 900 individuals, have registered with local councils as having no where to live.

Some are homeless because sponsorships have broken down, others because they have been in the UK for more than six months and don't have anywhere else to go. The figure is likely to be an underestimate, as not all councils provided figures."

==
======

Disclaimer:

Note: All rights reserved. No part of this book, ebook or manuscript or associated published or unpublished works may be copied, reproduced or transmitted by any means, electronic, mechanical, photocopying or otherwise, without the prior written permission of the author.

Copyright: Bob Able 2024

The author asserts the moral right under the Copyright, Design and Patents Act 1988 to be identified as the author of this work. This is a work of fiction, Any similarities between any persons, living or dead and the characters in this work is purely co-incidental.

The author accepts no claims in relation to this work.

Cover photo: by Cater Yang on Unsplash

About the Author:

Bob Able is a bestselling writer of popular memoirs, fiction and thrillers. He describes himself as a 'part time ex-pat' splitting his time between his homes in coastal Spain and 'darkest Norfolk' in the UK.

His memoir **'Spain Tomorrow'** was rated as the **third most popular travel book** by Amazon in September 2020 and continues to top the charts. With the sequel **'More Spain Tomorrow'**, followed by **'Third Helpings of Spain Tomorrow'**, these charming lighthearted insights into his life continue to amuse readers.

All his books are available as ebooks and paperbacks and can be found by entering 'Bob Able books' in the search bar.

If you like Bob Able's distinctive writing style and would like to read more of his work, here is a little more information......

Stop Press! *Enter 'Bob Able books' on Amazon for details! ....*

'Poo, Power and Politics' now published as an ebook and a paperback

'Sarah's Kitchen' now published as an ebook and a paperback

'Dicky And The Dame' is just released - *see free sample below!*

Bob Able writes with a lighthearted touch and does not use graphic descriptions of sex or violence in his books, that is not his style. He prefers to leave that sort of thing to the reader's imagination.

He has produced a new series of lighthearted thrillers which will amuse as well as captivate readers. They are ideal light reads to take on holiday. The **Bobby Bassington Stories** include:

'Bobbie And The Spanish Chap',
'Bobbie And The Crime-Fighting Auntie',
'Bobbie And The Wine Trouble'
And **'Auntie Caroline's Last Case'**

All these books can be read on their own, although if you read them as a series, **'Auntie Caroline's Last Case'** draws all the strings together and completes the tales of the lives of the characters we meet along the way.

Early reviewers had suggested that these stories would make an engaging TV series and of course Bob would be pleased to hear from television companies and promoters to explore that option!

His fictional novels include:

'**Double Life Insurance**' a fast moving but lighthearted thriller, where Bobbie Bassington first makes an appearance, fresh out of university:
'**No Point Running**' which is set in the world of horse racing and car theft in the 1970's before mobile phones and the internet:
'**The Menace Of Blood**', which is about inheritance, not gore, and the sequel
'**No Legacy of Blood**'.
They are all engaging thrillers, with a touch of romance and still with that gentle, signature Bob Able humour.

His semi-fictional memoir '**Silke The Cat, My Story**', written with his friend and wine merchant, Graham Austin and Silke the Cat herself, is completely different. Silke is a real cat, she lives today in the Costa Blanca, and her travels, which she recounts in this amusing book, really happened (also available as an audio book).

Contact:

bobable693@gmail.com
This is a 'live email address' and is monitored by Bob himself, so do not expect automated replies ... Bob hates that sort of impersonal thing.

You can find details of how to buy all Bob's books and also follow him at:
www.amazon.com/author/bobable

Or just enter '**Bob Able books**' on the Amazon site or Google and the full list should appear.

==
=======

To thank you for reading The Smug, here is an extract from Bob Able's new book 'Dicky & The Dame' available as a paperback or an ebook on Amazon now:-

DICKY & THE DAME

Introduction:-

This story is set in 1963 and although it is a work of fiction, whilst some names have been changed, all the historical context and references are accurate, as far can be reasonably established.

It is astonishing to think that 'conscription', in the form of National Service, bought in after the Second World War, only came to an end in 1963, when the last troops were 'demobbed'. Their service is often forgotten but it is worth revisiting the privations and the danger they faced and the losses they sustained. We owe them a debt of gratitude alongside the 'regular' soldiers, airmen and sailors who actually applied for jobs in the forces of their own free will at that time. Many of the conscripts had to put careers on hold, had family lives disrupted, and several found it hard to get work and reintegrate into civilian life after the upheaval of National Service.

By 1963, in civilian life, the British people generally were able to put the effects of the Second World War behind them, and a great spirit of optimism emerged. Life was improving for ordinary people, as well as the more privileged, in all sorts of ways. It was the start of an exciting era in history.

We follow Richard 'Dicky' Bourne as he leaves the Army behind, but not the effects, friendships and attitudes the era of National Service typified. From watching the building of the Berlin Wall whilst still a soldier, to returning to live with his sister in sleepy suburbia, Dicky's life certainly changes. But before he can settle down and look for a job, he has to find out who the girl involved in the car crash is, and engineer a way to meet her again. But she comes from a social class he could never hope to penetrate, and even in 1963, there are seemingly insurmountable barriers to overcome to launch his career.

Chapter 1
Demob day 1963

The last group of those called up for National Service were assembled for one final parade before their commanding officer, ahead of being released from their duties.

Colonel Reginald 'Tiger' Hampton mounted the small raised dais and prepared to address his men for the last time.

It was an emotional moment. It was the last time the Colonel, or all his military underlings could be rude to the men standing before them, with impunity. But more than that, it marked the end of an era.

'Ahem!' began the Colonel. 'Stand them "at ease", Sergeant Major,' and as the men relaxed a little, he prepared to deliver his last speech to the final intake of National Servicemen.

'Of course,' he began, 'working with a bunch of unwilling, ill-disciplined, lazy, unco-operative, and slow-witted twerps like you was never going to be the sort of commission a military man such as myself would choose, but for Queen and Country, and all that ... Anyway, I shall not detain you long. Some of you have what might loosely be described as "careers" to return to, although reading through the notes earlier, I can't say the life you choose appeals to me much. I accept that we must have farmers and clergymen, I suppose, but some of you rabble seem to be returning to civvy street as book-keepers, lawyers and fiction writers, and even poets. Up to you, of course, how you spend your time, but do we really need those last mentioned? I mean, poets? Ah, well, the world is a very different place now and we all have to adapt to it, I suppose. But I want to leave you with one last thought as you finally walk away. The military life may seem a little constraining to those of you with a literary bent, or maybe the other sort of bent that poets seem to like, but at its heart it turns out good men and true, who are prepared to respect the traditions of honour and service and do their best for their fellow man. Without such men the country we all love would be vulnerable to all sorts of bally nonsense, and before you know it we should have communists and discontent on every street corner. Poets aside, for a moment, I'm sure that is not the sort of England any of us, if we examine our hearts, really want to live in, and the old traditional values must be upheld …'

As he finished, some time later, Private 'Dicky' Bourne blew a quiet raspberry under his breath, and as the parade was dismissed for the last time, he and Private Hamish Swinney made their way back to the barracks to collect their belongs for the journey home.

-oOo-

'What are you going to do first, Hamish?' asked Dicky.

'You mean whan I sober up?' growled the amiable Scot. 'Ah shall have tay visit ma tailor, and get him to take in some of ma trews. I've a waistline now, thanks to all the starvation and running aboot we had tay do in yon camp.'

'Oh, it wasn't really so bad, was it? At least we got three square meals a day and we didn't actually have to shoot anyone.'

'Ah suppose yeh right, but I canna say I'll miss it. What aboot you, young Dicky? Wha does the future look like for you?'

'Oh, I'll get by, I guess. I'm going to try my luck in London, and see if I can get a Literary Agent to take me on, or maybe get a job with a publisher or something.'

'D'ya have anywhere tay live?'

'Not exactly, but my sister said I can sleep at her house for up to a month while I find something more permanent.'

'You'll no consider coming away to the Highlands wi me then? I ken ye said no last time ah asked, but the offer stands, if ye like.'

'That is very kind of you, Hamish, and life in a Scottish castle does sound rather fascinating, but I think I need the hustle and bustle of a London filled with artistic types and that sort of thing around me. I feel I could write something useful in that environment, and things are so different since we went in for National Service. I feel the world is opening up before us.'

'Wheel the offer stands if ye change yer mind, Dicky. I shall miss ye.'

'I'll miss you too, Hamish,' said Dicky, and as they rounded the corner of an accommodation block and stood in the seclusion of its shadow, the two retiring National Servicemen wrapped each other in a not unmanly, back-slapping embrace.

-oOo-

Standing beside the main road outside in drizzle was unpleasant, but essential for Dicky, as he peered hopefully at each black, two-door, Austin A30 that trundled past.

He knew that the only distinguishing mark separating the one he sought from the other, apparently identical, little cars which seemed so prevalent amongst the London traffic, was a stylised, colourful cartoon flower his sister had painted on the boot of her elderly vehicle. But of course, by the time that came into view the car would have passed by.

His only hope was to make himself as conspicuous as he could amongst the stationary and trudging masses on foot, moving in waves like the great herds of Africa, this way and that, on the pavement by the railway station entrance. His sister was not known for her punctuality, it had to be said, but Dicky hoped that on this day of days, as the rain fell a little harder, she would at least make an effort. He hoped his large military-issue kit-bag would also make it easier for his sister to spot him and occasionally he moved it around on the edge of the pavement to ensure it remained visible.

At last with an almost apologetic 'toot' a tired and somewhat faded, black Austin shuddered to a halt beside him. His sister's head, with its blizzard of curls, appeared from within the tiny car.

'Come on then, Richard. I haven't got all day!' she bellowed cheerfully, and indicated that Dicky should use the passenger door, which was facing the traffic rather than the pavement, to manhandle his heavy bag onto the back seat, as the stream of cars and trucks crawled past. Several taxi drivers sounded their horns when having to detour around the door and Dicky's protruding rump, as he struggled to force his kit-bag into the vehicle.

Replacing the folding seat back in an approximation of its original position as it leaned toward the bulging kit-bag, Dicky threw himself into the car and slammed the door.

'It just would rain, wouldn't it, Sophie,' wheezed Dicky above the screech of the windscreen wipers. 'Been lovely all week, but now this!'

'It's the Dicky Bourne luck,' smiled his sister, adjusting her ample frame on the small seat and putting on the trafficator to indicate her intention to edge out into the busy road. 'You bring all sorts of problems wherever you go. You always have.'

'Nice to see you too, Sis,' smiled Dicky, just as a large Bentley, sounding its horn imperiously, crunched into the rear nearside wing of the A30, and following the incident, all forward motion ceased.

-o0o-

'Whatever happened, Jarvis? Will this take long?'

From the back seat of the gleaming Bentley the silvery voice of the only thing more glamorous than the elegant car reached the chauffeur's ears as he began to open the door.

'A little black car got in the way, Miss Camilla, and I'm afraid we have bumped it,' he offered in his best, if somewhat nasal, imitation of the correct modulated speech he had heard on the radio.

'Bumped it? Oh, dear, I hope we are not going to be late. Mother will be at the Savoy by now, waiting.'

'If you will just excuse me a moment, miss. I believe I can soon get them to remove that wreck from our path. I doubt there is much dammidge to speak of.'

But there was damage, and although not severe, there would be paperwork to attend to, no doubt.

Dicky was out of the car in a trice and inspecting the dented rear corner of the Austin and the scratch on the paint above the bumper of the Bentley when Jarvis joined him.

'You could see I was pulling out, I had the trafficator on!' exclaimed Sophie, thrusting herself through the growing crowd of onlookers gathering around the scene.

'She pulled roight aht into 'is path, she did!' observed one of the onlookers, pausing from his duties selling newspapers at the roadside.

'Clumsy kah!' exclaimed another.

'Yon chauffeur 'ad is nose so far in the bloomin' air, 'ee weren't looking where 'ee was goin', few ask me!' added a passer-by helpfully.

'Snow body 'urt, mind' added a spotty youth in school uniform, who received a sharp tap on the head from the woman who held his hand, for his intervention.

'Come away, young 'Erbert,' said the woman. 'Or there's more where that came from!'

In all the jostling, had it not been for her singular ability to turn heads, Camilla would have been just one more face in the throng. But, though petite, such was the effect of her dazzling personality and immaculate appearance, that a path was cleared for her through the little crowd and she glided, unmolested, to the point of the impact, seemingly effortlessly.

She spoke but one word, but it was enough.

Apart from a 'Coo!' from 'Erbert as he drank in her slim legs under her stylish dress and the wide-brimmed, yellow hat that shaded her large green eyes, the little knot of onlookers fell silent.

'Jarvis?' she said.

-oOo-

Chapter 2
An accidental meeting

Titled ladies, whether they have inherited their status as the daughters of countless Earls, or, as in the present case, by services to the world of film and theatre, always seem to be able to find a good table at the Savoy.

As the sole occupant of the table set for luncheon, just the right distance from its neighbours, Dame Amelia Barron-Zukor sat in splendid isolation toying with a wide-brimmed glass of champagne.

She was becoming impatient.

She glanced at her elegant little gold wristwatch (a final birthday present from her second husband, just before he died) and sighed. Although, when you came right down to it, she had no other pressing appointments, Dame Amelia always gave the impression of being terrifically busy. It had kept film directors on their toes and made mere scriptwriters hurry on with their alterations when progress was delayed on any of the glittering cinematic extravaganzas in which she had appeared. Although all that was now long behind her, the mannerisms she adopted then still made cameo appearances today.

An attentive waiter, standing nearby, misinterpreting the action and imagining this grand lady was in need of his services, hurried to her side to ask if he could be of assistance. She dismissed him with a wave of the slim hand that had once enchanted screen lovers and drawn sighs from enraptured audiences, and glanced once again at her wristwatch.

The waiter caught sight of the large diamond ring on that elegant hand and decided that he was indeed in the presence of some sort of royalty.

'Sorry, Mummy,' said a voice behind him as he moved out of the path of one of his colleagues, directing a trim young woman into the presence of the great lady.

'Camilla! Where on earth have you been?' The unmistakable liquid tones, once so famous and much emulated by several later starlets, gently chided. As the new arrival took her seat, that wonderful voice melted the romantic hearts of the two waiters looking on.
Both had recently seen a rerun of one of Dame Amelia's early films in the 'Golden Days of Cinema' festival held at the flea-pit nearby, in-between their shifts in the dining room.

-oOo-

Dicky wasn't really listening.

Sophie had been talking nonstop, and recounting the little accident from her viewpoint yet again.

'I only hope Gerald doesn't change his mind when he hears about this. I was so looking forward to having a new Mini.'

'New Mini?' said Dicky, taking an interest in this new twist in the tired story of the bump outside the railway station.

'Haven't you been listening, Dicky? I told you. Gerald has promised we can buy a new Mini in time for the winter if we can keep the old car going until then, and if we don't have to spend any money on it in the meantime. Gerald has been promoted and is due to get a bonus from the company, as I was explaining.'

'Sorry, m'yes. That will be very nice. But I've already offered to pay for the repairs ...'

'I know you have, and it was very sweet of you. It doesn't matter about the dent on our car, that is just one more for the collection, but it is how much that pompous chauffeur will try to extract for the scratch on the Bentley bumper that worries me.'

The reason Dicky was not really listening was because his head was full of the image of the vision of paradise who had stepped out of the rear of the Bentley and came to stand beside him inspecting the damage. He hadn't be able to think about anything else since.

He had heard the chauffeur call her 'Miss Camilla' as he assured her he would not be long in exchanging names and addresses with Sophie. After arranging to call round to the house when, as he put it, the extent of the "dammidge" had been assessed and a cost estimate prepared, he had guided the lovely girl back into the car.

But it was the smile she gave him as she turned to get into the car that would be haunting Dicky's dreams from now on. She was designed, he decided, precisely to his personal requirements, and was so perfect, it was as though he had drawn up the blueprints for her creation himself.
He had no doubt that she was the best candidate to become his partner in life that he had ever encountered. Dicky did not fall for girls by the dozen like some chaps he knew, but this was actually it, he was sure. He just had to figure out a way to get to know her.

'Sophie, why don't you give me the address, and I'll go and see the chauffeur fellow and see if we can come to an arrangement before he turns up with his blasted estimate. If I can square him, Gerald need never know about this little accident.'

'Oh, would you, Dicky? I would be most grateful. You see Petal is getting rather old and I really would love a new Mini.'

'Petal?' asked Dicky.

'Yes, that is her name. From the number-plate … PTL 832 … 'Petal' you see. Silly isn't it, but that is what she has always been called ever since we bought her new at Christmas time in 1952.'

-oOo-

To read more of this and all Bob Able's books just enter 'Bob Able books' on Amazon or Google or follow this link to his latest books:-

https://tinyurl.com/yebx4mus

Printed in Great Britain
by Amazon